A Harlequin Romance

OTHER
Harlequin Romances
by NAN ASQUITH

Many of these titles are available at your local bookseller,
or through the Harlequin Reader Service.

For a free catalogue listing all available Harlequin Romances,
send your name and address to:

HARLEQUIN READER SERVICE,
M.P.O. Box 707, Niagara Falls, N.Y. 14302
Canadian address: Stratford, Ontario, Canada.

or use order coupon at back of book.

THE
GIRL FROM ROME

by

NAN ASQUITH

HARLEQUIN BOOKS   TORONTO
WINNIPEG

Original hard cover edition published in 1973
by Mills & Boon Limited.

© Nan Asquith 1973

SBN 373-01734-0

Harlequin edition published November 1973

Printed in Canada

CHAPTER ONE

IT was the last night of the last week of the season. Tomorrow the tour party would fly home to England and at the end of the week the office of the Dana Tourist Agency would close down until spring. Some of the staff would be going on to other holiday jobs; to winter sports centres or to the Canary Isles. Jane was the only one remaining in Rome for the winter.

It was Gino who had persuaded her to stay.

'Do not go back to England in October,' he had said. 'Do not leave me, Jane. I shall be desolate. We have had such a—how do you say?—good time together. It has been the most happy summer of my life.' He had taken her two hands in his. 'Tell me that it has been the same for you.'

Jane could certainly say that. But then, to date, her summers hadn't been especially happy. Until the time she had left her dull job with the firm of exporters in the City with whom she had been working and joined the Dana Tourist Agency. On the strength of her Italian, which was fluent and extensive, she had been sent to the Rome office the following year and suddenly everything was changed. The job was full-time and she worked long hours and was always short on sleep, but living in Rome was such a fabulous experience she felt sometimes that she would never be the same person again. Then she met Gino and that made everything perfect.

She turned to wave encouragingly at the tour party who were coming up behind her before leading them across the square. Jane thought, as she glanced round, that the Piazza Navona had never looked more beautiful than tonight. The shutters of the tall stucco-fronted houses stood open and the apartments behind them were gold-lit stage sets, magical and mysterious. The waters of the great Fountain of the

5

Rivers lifted silvery cascades towards the velvet blue of the Rome night sky while the massive front of St. Agnes in Agone glowed in the floodlighting.

The Piazza was crowded with people; with holiday-makers and sightseers, with family parties and scampering children; with lovers who strolled hand in hand past artists who displayed their works on the pavement and hippies who sprawled on the ground, strumming guitars or endeavoured to sell the trinkets and souvenirs spread out before them.

As the party gathered round her Jane raised her voice so that all could hear.

'The Square we are now standing in is called the Piazza Navona. It is entirely characteristic of Baroque Rome. It is built on the ruins of the Stadium of Domitian. The fountain you see behind you is known as the Fountain of the Rivers and was designed by Gianlorenzo Bernini. You will note ...' and she went on to give description and details of the architecture.

From the fountain they moved to the Church and then to the Obelisk. Jane went on reciting her piece, answering questions, before moving on again. She glanced at her wrist-watch. It was after eleven. Fabio would be waiting with the coach in the side street just beyond the Piazza at half past eleven. When she had seen the last of the party on to the coach she would be free to meet Gino as arranged. People said that life in Rome didn't begin until after eleven, and that definitely applied to Jane. She was seldom free during the day, for the staff had little time off and no actual days, nor did the couriers work a shift system. In consequence any social life they had started late in the evening.

Someone was speaking to her, asking yet another question. With her mind half on Gino and half on the last rounding up of the party, she answered absently,

'Yes. The building next to the Church is the Pamphili Palace, built by Pope Innocent X Pamphili and designed by Bernini.'

A voice said,

'*Rainaldi*. The architect was Girolamo Rainaldi.'

Jane turned abruptly, feeling her face flush at the error she had just made. A tall dark man was staring at her across the heads of the people in between. He nodded and repeated in the same laconic voice,

'Rainaldi.'

She swallowed.

'Th-thank you. Yes, of course.' She looked at the upturned faces surrounding her. 'I'm sorry, I—made a mistake. This palace was designed by Girolamo Rainaldi.' She paused and then added, 'Now, if you'll please follow me we will go to where the coach is waiting to take you back to your hotel.'

She started off briskly and with purpose. Unfortunately on her way she had to pass the tall figure still standing, hands in fawn slacks, at the back of the tour party. She avoided looking at him, but to her dismay he turned and walked along beside her, saying, 'I hope you don't do that too often.'

She gave him a quick sideways glance, registering a dark unsmiling face, a deep-cut mouth and a determined jaw.

'Do? Oh yes, I see.' She could feel her chin tilting skywards in an attempt at dignity. 'I—it's never happened before. I just wasn't thinking.'

'Obviously. But if you're attempting to educate the ignorant it's as well to keep your mind on the job and make sure your facts are correct.'

'Thank you.' Jane's voice was cold despite the anger welling up inside her. Only the restraints of the job kept her from answering sarcastically. She gave him another quick look and sudden doubt prompted her to add, 'Are you a member of the party—I don't seem to remember seeing you before?'

He gave a short ejaculation which wasn't quite a laugh.

'Heaven forbid! I've never been on a conducted tour yet and I don't intend to start now.'

7

She stopped dead in her tracks.

'You mean—you were just *listening*? And you b-butted in like that—interfering—making me look an absolute f-fool?' She found herself stammering with indignation.

He said mildly, 'You made a wrong statement. I had to put things right.' He jerked his head in the direction of the figures pattering along behind them. 'Otherwise those poor souls would be going around with a lot of misguided ideas.'

She said explosively,

'I think you've got an absolute nerve! Would you go away, please. You don't belong with this tour.'

His eyes were a dark slatey grey beneath straight black brows.

'For which I'm deeply thankful. Don't forget—keep your mind on the job. Goodnight,' and he wheeled away, hands still in pockets, stride lengthening but not hastening.

Jane took a deep breath in an effort to restore her equilibrium. Hateful, infuriating man! She was glad to see the back of him.

She managed to calm down enough to see the party safely on to the coach, to give Fabio some last-minute instructions and to assure everyone she would be at the Leonardo da Vinci airport next morning to see them off. Then, with a last wave of her hand, she turned and walked back towards the restaurant where she was to meet Gino.

He would be there already, she felt sure, but he never seemed to mind waiting. Italians didn't fuss about time like Englishmen. That was one of the nice things about them, among all the other things. Like being warm-hearted and gay and marvellously good-looking and attentive and demonstrative and interested in you as a girl. Jane had never had a real boy-friend until she met Gino. In England there had been a few dates, but they hadn't meant very much and she had been too busy looking after her mother, who was an invalid, and trying to hold down her job with the export firm, to have much time for members of the opposite sex. Her father had died when she was ten and her mother had brought up Jane and her sister on very limited means. A year after Rosemary had married and gone to live in Leamington, their mother had fallen ill. The three of them had been very close and for over a year they tried to reassure one another that Mrs. Roper was going to get better, but it didn't happen that way.

After she died Jane left the job in the City and went to stay for a few weeks with Rosemary and Bill, and then, when she felt better, she returned to London to share a flat with a girl cousin, and that was when she started with the Dana Travel Agency. Coming to Rome and meeting Gino had been like coming out of shadows into sunlight. It wasn't surprising that she was so much in love with him.

The Toscano Restaurant was on the far side of the Piazza Navona. Its terraces were surrounded by greenery; small box trees in tubs and vines twisting up painted trelliswork, and geraniums and petunias in pots. A few late diners were still sitting out, for although it was mid-October the night was almost as warm as June. Jane peered through the trellis, wondering at which table Gino would be sitting, but there was no sign of him; she had arrived first after all. She was about to go through the opening when she heard a voice call 'Jane—Jane!' and swinging round in the direction of the sound walked smack into someone. Two hands came out to steady her and glancing up in quick apology Jane found herself staring into the frowning face of the dark stranger of a short while ago.

'Careful!' His voice was abrupt, almost impatient.

She jerked free.

'I'm sorry.'

'Oh—it's you again.' He stared down at her, then gave a quick glance round. 'Where's the retinue got to?'

She said stiffly,

'The tour party have gone back to their hotel.' She moved away. 'Excuse me, please.'

He gave a small inclination of his head and stepped back, and at the same moment Gino appeared, both hands out-

9

stretched towards her.

'Jane! Darling, I am so sorry that I am late,' and catching hold of her two hands he leaned forward and kissed her on her lips.

'It's all right. I—I've only just come.' Jane was vaguely aware of a tall figure hovering somewhere in the background and for a second, as she turned to walk into the Toscano, she met the stranger's grave dark glance and then he was gone.

'What man is that with whom you speak?' Gino demanded as he sat down at the table with Jane. He frowned. 'He is one of your tour—no? I am jealous of him. Does he fall in love with you?'

Jane laughed out loud at the mere idea.

'Oh, Gino! I never set eyes on him until half an hour ago. He's a perfectly horrible man—rude and interfering,' and she went on to tell Gino what had happened.

'*Lui e bruto*. To speak so to Jane—Jane *si bella*—*si gentile*!' He shook his head smilingly. 'But I am glad he does not love you.'

'Far from it,' Jane smiled back, thinking how handsome Gino was. He wasn't as dark as most Italians; his hair was a crisp almost curly brown and his eyes were brown too, but bright and sparkling and full of golden lights. His skin was smooth and golden and although he was not tall he was well proportioned and had a compactly muscular look.

Neither of them wanted anything to eat, only some wine to drink. Across the table Gino clasped her hand in his.

'It is *finito*—your work? No more the drivings round—the starings—*le lezione*?'

'No. Tomorrow the tour party flies back to England.'

Gino sighed contentedly.

'But not my Jane. You cannot know how happy you have made me, *cara*, that you stay here in Rome. Now there will be no winter. It will be summer every day.'

'I shall have to get another job.' She looked at him. 'Did you—I suppose you haven't heard of anything yet?'

10

'Yes. I am hopeful. A friend of mine—what you call a business acquaintance?—he has need of someone who can translate well. For *la correspondenza*, you understand?'

Jane nodded.

'Yes. How super—it sounds exactly what I could do—the same as I did in England. What happens? Do I go to see him—them?'

'I will give you the address—I have it,' and Gino searched in the pockets of his thin dark suit. 'It is here. If you will write or telephone a time will be arranged for the meeting.'

Jane glanced down at the card inscribed with a name and address.

'You are kind, Gino. Thank you—thank you terrifically.'

He frowned.

'Terr-iff-ic-allee? What is that?'

'Oh, you know. Greatly. Enormously. Tremendously.'

A smile lit his brown face.

'I understand. I love you terr-iff-ic-allee. That is right?'

Jane looked away.

'I hope so.'

'And you love me terr-iff-ic-allee also?'

She stared down at the check tablecloth without answering.

'Please,' Gino insisted, his fingers tight on hers. 'Please say that it is true, Jane, that you love me.'

'I can't say it here, just like that.'

'Then we will go somewhere quiet—private, where we can speak as we wish.' He glanced round impatiently for the waiter. 'I will pay the check.'

Jane hesitated, shaking her head.

'I don't think I should go anywhere now, Gino. It's late —well after midnight, and I have to be up very early in the morning to go to the airport.'

'But, Jane, *cara dolce amante*—we have had no time—it is that you arrive only short time ago. Let us go somewhere —I have the car.'

11

She was longing to stay with Gino, but she knew that if she did it would be very late before she got back to the small apartment that she shared with Meg, one of the other girls working at the Dana Agency. She still had her job to do, the party to see safely off to England in the morning, a long day to be spent at the office, clearing up papers and files ready for the move out at the end of the week.

'Honestly, Gino, I don't think I can. But there'll be other evenings—other times we can be—be together.'

'We could go dancing,' Gino said coaxingly. 'There is that little place in the Trastevere—the one with the garden that you like so much. We will sit and talk—I will hold you in my arms to the music and tell you that I love you terr-if-ic-allee and you will tell me so in return—yes? Please say "yes", Jane.'

She bit her lip. It was so tempting. The little *trattoria* Gino had mentioned—the Antica Ranieri—was a favourite place, with its own small garden where they had dined and danced several times. It was part of the magic of this summer—a summer Jane never wanted to say goodbye to. So many happy days they had shared. Like the one when she and Gino had walked hand in hand through empty streets and deserted squares because it was a Sunday and the hottest day of the year and it seemed as if everybody else had left Rome. Jane hadn't been able to because she was meeting an incoming plane at six o'clock and so Gino had stayed with her, and it had been an unforgettable day, framed in sunlight.

She sighed.

'I—can't, Gino. I want to, very much, but I have to put the job first—until I'm finished with it.'

'Ah, Jane, you are so English—so prim and conscientious. Like a little schoolmistress, knowing what is good for you to do—and for me also.' He shrugged. 'We shall change all that—you will see.' He handed the hovering waiter some lire. 'Come, then.'

'I'm sorry,' Jane said. 'You do understand, though, don't you?'

Gino shook his head.

'No, I do not understand. I do not understand how anyone must always put duty before pleasure. But that is the British way, I think.' He took hold of her arm. 'Shall we go to the car—it is parked some little way?'

'No. It isn't worth the trouble. I can walk.'

'I will walk with you.'

The Via Flavia was no distance, just off the Via della Scrofa, and in no time at all they had reached the shabby stucco-fronted house where the apartment was situated.

Gino took her hands in his.

'Now we say *arrivederci*. But I will see you soon, *cara*. Telephone me at my office and tell me how you proceed with Signor Baldoni.'

'Yes, of course.'

'We will meet again when I hear from you.' Gino frowned, glancing away from her. 'I am not—certain of my plans at the moment. Some—some family arrangement. You understand? My mother, she returns from Forte de Marmi this week.'

'I understand,' Jane said. Gino, who spoke seldom of his family, had explained to Jane that his mother was a widow; that he and his brother Mario ran the family business which had to do with silk and textiles. Mario was married and throughout the hot Rome summer his wife Tina and the two children stayed at their holiday villa at Forte de Marmi with Signora Abetti. Several weekends Gino had driven down to be with them and once he had stayed a week, but when Jane saw him on his return he had told her it had all been 'too much family'.

Now all the family were returning to Rome for the winter. Soon I shall meet Signora Abetti, Jane thought. And Gino's brother and his wife and children, perhaps. I should like to do that—to know Gino's family.

Gino took her in an ardent embrace and kissed her,

13

murmuring endearments.

'I cannot live without you, Jane. You must know that.'

The arrival of one of the apartments' occupants who stopped and stared curiously at them caused Jane to break free. She said breathlessly,

'I must go, Gino. Goodnight, and thank you. I'll be in touch—about—about the job.'

'Yes. *Arrivederci*, darling.'

In the bleakly furnished room which Jane shared with Meg and which even the addition of their clothes and personal possessions did little to alleviate the starkness, Meg was in bed. She opened a sleepy eye to say yawningly,

'You're certainly living it up. How about that early call?'

'Don't worry, I'll make it,' Jane said. 'I'm sorry if I woke you.'

Meg turned over in the narrow divan bed which stood on the other side of the room from where Jane's was.

'I wasn't really asleep. It's been so noisy.'

It was always noisy in Rome, and you never really got used to it. The sound of the traffic never stopped until the dead of night, or rather, small hours of the morning. Until then there was the drone of car engines, the revving up of recalcitrant motors, the deafening blare of horns. When the windows were open, as they had been all summer, you could hear the echo of voices, singing, shouting, quarrelling; the bumble of innumerable T.V. sets from the other apartments, the cries of children, the thump of road-mending and always, from every corner of the city, the church bells, insistent and incessant.

As Jane set the alarm she thought that she would have to look for another apartment that week. This one, although far from luxurious, would be too big and too expensive for her on her own. A lot would depend on what the job with Signor Baldoni paid. *If* she got the job with Signor Baldoni. Oh well, time enough to think about all that tomorrow.

The next few days rushed away as there was so much to

do. The office had to be cleared of books and papers and all the documents relating to the Agency. The manager, Bill McLean, was going back to England to the London office; one of the girls was going to Austria for the winter sports later on. Meg, fair-haired, blue-eyed, was returning with Bill to England, for she was engaged to a boy in her home town of Sevenoaks and going to be married after Christmas. Only Jane was staying in Rome.

'Lucky you,' Meg said. 'Not that I'd want to remain here when Tony's waiting for me at home, but if I were footloose like you are I'd love to stay for the winter. Have you fixed a new job yet?'

'I'm going tomorrow for an interview with the firm that Gino told me about. I do hope I'm lucky—it sounds ideal.'

Meg smiled encouragingly. 'I'll keep my fingers crossed for you.'

The offices of Enrico Baldoni and Co. were in an imposing modern building, just off the Via Milano. Signor Baldoni himself was a short dark man in his early forties, effusive and charming and singularly unbusinesslike. He appeared to take it for granted that Jane had the necessary qualifications for the job of secretary-translator and took more interest in her previous work and her friendship with Gino than anything else. It made Jane slightly uncomfortable and she was at pains to stress her experience and references, not wanting to think that the post was being given to her solely through Gino's influence.

The salary was satisfactory and with her work permit being in order it was arranged that she would start work the following Monday week.

After much shaking of hands and several admiring compliments being paid to her by Signor Baldoni, Jane left the office and hurried to telephone the successful news to Gino.

'I am sorry, Signor Abetti is not here today,' a woman's voice informed Jane. 'I am sorry, I do not know if he will be here tomorrow. Is there a message you wish to leave for him?'

Jane was at a loss. She knew so little of Gino's private life. She had met him at a party and at once he had been attracted to her, as she was to him. They met frequently but haphazardly, due to the pressure of Jane's job with its irregular working hours. Usually Gino left a note at the Agency office with regard to their meeting and Jane would leave a similar one in return, which he would collect if he did not see her in person. He had early on given her the telephone number of his place of business but cautioned her not to ring him there unless he had particularly requested it. She did not know his actual home address except that it was somewhere near or on the Via Aurelia.

Once he had said,

'It is a large villa—very old. It belonged to my father's family for many years. Now it is closed up for the summer —there is only the gardener and his wife who caretake. I sleep there'—he had shrugged—'no more. Many times I am at the apartment of a friend in Rome—I stay with him for company.'

It was Friday. Tonight the Dana office closed up. If she could not get in touch with Gino today or tomorrow she would have to leave contacting him until Monday. Oh well, Jane thought philosophically, I can spend the weekend looking for a new apartment.

But when she got back to the Agency it was to find that Gino had left a message for her.

'Your boy-friend rang—could you meet him at nine o'clock this evening at the Toscano,' Meg said. She glanced enquiringly at Jane. 'Did you get the job?'

'Yes. Isn't it terrific? It's exactly what I want—and can do. Very modern offices—bright and airy—and they seem a nice firm.'

'I'm glad. That's super, Jane.'

Jane was glowing. Gino had telephoned. They were to meet that evening and she had got the new job. Everything was turning out in the most wonderful way possible.

Strolling into the Piazza Navona at nine o'clock to

wander leisurely in the direction of the Toscano Restaurant, with time to stop and stare, to enjoy the sightseers and the passers-by was much pleasanter than whirling round in charge of a party of tourists. Not that she hadn't enjoyed the latter's company and friendship, but it was nice to be free of responsibility for their enjoyment and welfare.

Now I can enjoy Rome, she thought. As if she hadn't. As if the days and the nights hadn't been the best ever.

She had arranged it so that she arrived at the meeting place six minutes after the appointed time. But, as before, Gino hadn't arrived.

Jane took a short walk round, gazed at some paintings being displayed by a tall young man with a red beard and a shock of red hair to match. They were little more than daubs, and she shook her head at his attempt at sales patter and walked on.

Still no Gino. Quarter of an hour late—twenty minutes. Another walk towards the great front of the church, to stare up at the twin towers outlined against the blue night sky. Back again to the Toscano, and Gino was half an hour late.

Should she go in and wait for him? But one thing Jane hated was to sit in a café unescorted—some predatory Italian was bound to attach himself to her. It was bad enough standing here, aware that the same young man had passed and repassed her, was now staring boldly and unabashed into her face.

She turned away and a voice said,

'Hello. I thought I recognised you.'

Jane glanced up quickly and saw a tall black-haired figure looking down at her. She blinked and then remembered. The interfering man of a few nights ago. She had never thought to be glad to see him again, but at that moment someone so English—so austere and coolly indifferent in voice and manner was an immediate reassurance. At least his greeting had sent the would-be admirer on his way.

'Oh, hello.'

'Has your date stood you up?'

He had a genius for saying the wrong thing, for making the sort of remark that caused her immediate annoyance.

'I don't think so.'

One black eyebrow lifted sceptically.

'No? He must be on the tardy side—you've been hanging around for quite a while. I was watching you.'

She was furious, on the verge of making an angry retort, but something stopped her; a reluctance to send him on his way before Gino arrived. At the moment he was a refuge, albeit a disagreeable one. She said coldly,

'Really? Haven't you something better to do?'

He shrugged.

'Actually, no. I'm just killing time. As you seem to be.' He glanced round. 'Where are they, by the way?'

'They?'

'The flock. You're a shepherdess without your sheep to-night.'

'As far as I know they're all safely back in England. The tours have ended for the season.'

'But you've not gone with them? Are you staying on in Rome?'

Her glance went past him, searching for Gino—looking for the familiar brown head.

'Yes.'

His look followed hers.

'I don't think he's coming. He'd surely never dare turn up this late.' He saw Jane's expression and added, 'Let me buy you a drink.'

She hesitated, not wanting to prolong the conversation, yet oddly reluctant to be left on her own or to walk away.

He saw the hesitation and put the tips of his fingers under her elbow.

'We might as well kill time together,' he said.

18

CHAPTER TWO

THEY sat down at a table at the back of the terrace, Jane somewhat uncertainly, the stranger with the air of frowning preoccupation which seemed a part of him.

'By the way, my name's Vance Morley. What would you like to drink?'

'Oh, coffee. Just coffee, thank you.'

He lifted a black eyebrow.

'Sure?' and at Jane's quick nod gave an order to the waiter who had promptly appeared upon the scene. He was the one who had so often served Gino and herself, and now his glance held both curiosity and reproach as he greeted her with the warmth of an old acquaintance. When he had disappeared towards the rear of the restaurant Vance Morley said,

'I won't ask if you come here often. You obviously do. Surely it's not part of the tour itinerary?' His voice was slow, almost drawling and held a mocking note.

'No.' Jane was angry with herself for accepting this annoying man's invitation. Why was she sitting here with him like this? It was the last thing she had intended to do. But she had been so worried over Gino's non-appearance that she had allowed herself to be manoeuvred into the situation.

There was a pause while they waited for the drinks to arrive. Vance Morley made no attempt at small talk and Jane herself sat silent because she had no wish to enter into conversation with him. But, glancing from under her lashes at the man opposite, she did wonder why he had invited her in the first place, for he sat back in his chair, long legs outstretched, staring into space with the same look of aloof preoccupation she had noticed in him before.

As if aware of her look his dark glance came back to regard her and he said unsmilingly,

19

'You didn't tell me your name.'

'Jane—Jane Roper.'

The waiter arrived with the drinks and when he had placed the cup of *capuccino* and the glass of lager on the table and departed Vance Morley said,

'Tell me, Jane Roper, why are you staying on in Rome if the tourist season is over, as you say?'

'It is for the particular company I work for. But many of the larger ones remain open all year. The Dana Agency is only small, although it's quite well known.'

'You haven't answered my question. Have you got another job to go to?'

'Yes.' She added, 'Actually I don't start there until a week on Monday.'

'What doing?'

'I'm to be a translator with a firm of architects who build hotels.'

He stared at her over the rim of his glass.

'That sounds very grand. You were lucky to get another job so quickly.'

'Yes. A—friend helped me—gave me the introduction.'

'The young Italian I saw you with the other evening? Is he the one you were supposed to be meeting tonight?'

Jane's round chin tilted defensively.

'Are you always so curious about people you've just met?'

He shrugged wide shoulders. Now she came to look at him more closely she could see he was older than she had thought, in his early thirties and good-looking despite the moody frown. His dark hair had blue-black lights in it, his nose was straight and commanding, the firm mouth had a full lower lip above a deeply cleft chin. The odd thing was that although he had asked so many questions Jane still couldn't feel he had any personal interest in her.

'Not often. But you roused my speculation the other evening, trotting round that crowd of people like a small sheepdog, reeling off a spiel of information, some of it incorrect, and then rushing away to herd them off somewhere else.'

'You put me in an invidious position, correcting me like that in front of everyone.'

The faintest glimmer of a smile lit his dark face.

'I suppose they thought you were infallible until then? That would be too much to ask of someone so young and inexperienced.'

Jane felt like getting up and walking away there and then. Instead she said angrily,

'I *am* experienced. And the error I made was a slip of the tongue, as I told you, not because I had the facts wrong.'

'How old are you?'

'Really! What on earth has that to do with you? I—I'm twenty-one.'

He nodded.

'Just as I thought. Young and—I won't say foolish—untried; green, perhaps.'

She said stiffly but politely, reaching for her shoulder bag, 'I must be going now. Thank you for the coffee.'

He gestured as if to restrain her.

'I'm sorry, I'm afraid I appeared rude—I didn't mean to be. Don't rush away. Have another coffee—or a drink?'

Jane fully intended to leave. She was annoyed and indignant with Vance Morley, but when the slate-grey eyes looked into hers, so direct and imperative, something in his glance caused her to sit down on the chair again.

'Good. I'm forgiven? Let me order you another *capuccino*. Cigarette? No?' He took one for himself from a battered packet.

'I could ask you some questions for a change,' Jane said. 'What are you doing here—are you on holiday, or have you got a job?'

'Neither. I'm—for want of a better word—marking time.'

'Waiting for someone, you mean?'

He shook his head, his expression sober.

'Waiting to move on. When I've made up my mind to go,

21

that is.'

'Where to?' Jane asked. In spite of herself she was interested. Something about his frowning looks, his indifference, intrigued her. And the conversation kept her mind off Gino and the anxiety of what had happened to him and why no message had come.

'To Corfu.'

She sighed.

'Oh, nice! I've never been there, but I hope to one day. What are you going there for?'

He stubbed the end of the cigarette out with an abrupt movement.

'I'm going to visit—relatives.'

'Do they live on the island?'

'I see what you mean—about all the questions. They get monotonous. And I'm a particularly boring subject. Let's talk about something else.'

'We don't know each other well enough to have a real conversation,' Jane said. 'It has to be question and answer.'

'We could talk about Rome.'

'Yes, we could do that.' Jane gave another sigh. 'I could tell you that I think it's the most wonderful city I've ever lived in.'

'And you've lived in so many? I'm sorry, that's not a question. I could say the same—and I've lived and worked half across the world.'

Jane looked at him.

'Now I want to ask you where—and what were you doing?'

He shook his head.

'Not allowed. We're only permitted to compare notes on Rome.'

In the end it turned into a discussion—quick and vital, and Jane, who thought she knew Rome because she had spent a summer working in the city and studied its history and conducted parties of holidaymakers from one historic monument to another until she was familiar with every

22

street and piazza, realised that compared with Vance Morley she scarcely knew Rome at all.

She had forgoten about time until she glanced at her wrist-watch and said, in amazement,

'Heavens, how late it is! I must go.'

'Eleven o'clock? That's early for Rome. Look, what about something to eat? You must be hungry—I know I am. It's hardly fair to the restaurant to have sat so long over two *capuccini* and two lagers.'

She shook her head.

'No, really. Thank you, but I—I have to get back to my apartment.' She hesitated. 'There—there may be a message waiting for me.'

'I see. Your Italian friend.' He stood up. 'Let me walk along with you.'

'Please don't bother—it's no way.'

'I've nothing better to do. Sorry, that sounds rude again. I'm grateful to you for helping me to pass the time so pleasantly.'

When he had paid for the drinks they turned and walked out of the Piazza Navona into the Via del Salvatore and on to the Via della Scrofa. Here in the maze of streets lying between the Via della Scrofa and the Via de Corso was Jane's apartment.

As they crossed the street the man at her side turned his head to say, 'Is your—friend the reason you're staying on in Rome?'

Jane glanced quickly up at him.

'I thought we'd stopped asking questions.'

He frowned.

'I admit I'm curious about you. I don't know why. It must be that wide-eyed, slightly vulnerable look. Probably very misleading. You must be capable and sensible or you wouldn't have held down your job with the Agency, much less talked yourself into a job over here. All the same, I hope you know something about this Italian—they're notorious charmers, for ever leading little English girls up the garden path and then fading out.'

'Thank you,' Jane said coolly. 'I happen to know Gino very well.'

'And his family? It's always wise to know the background of anyone one becomes romantically involved with. Especially if they happen to be a nationality other than one's own, and of a different religion.'

Jane forced her voice into lightness.

'Who said anything about being romantically involved?'

'No need for words. Don't forget, I saw you the other night, saw that lovers' greeting. You were positively starry-eyed—a dangerous state of affairs.'

Jane was thankful to see that they had reached the apartment building. She halted in her tracks and turned to say,

'Please don't waste your time giving me advice. Even if I needed some it's hardly likely I'd want it from a perfect stranger. I don't need any from anyone. Thank you for the coffee and for walking back with me. Goodnight.'

He looked down at her. He was a very tall man and Jane was a small girl. He said quietly,

'I've offended you. I'm sorry. Goodnight. I hope everything turns out well,' and with a casual lift of one hand he swung round and walked slowly away.

Well, Jane thought, climbing up the seventy-two steps that led to the two rooms she shared with Meg, what an exasperating man! Talking to her like some old uncle, giving her advice about Gino as if she were a silly moonstruck girl.

She was back before Meg, who had gone out with the other members of the Agency and some Italian friends for a farewell party. Jane would have gone too if it had not been for her arrangement with Gino. And then he had not arrived.

There was no message awaiting her, to explain his absence. She could only think that the return of his family from the coast had in some way altered his plans. He hadn't said *which* day they were returning to Rome; perhaps they had come back today and so delayed his coming to meet her?

She felt flat and empty. Talking to Vance Morley had passed the evening, but now, with Meg still out, there was a sense of anticlimax and despite herself, she thought of Vance's remarks about knowing more of Gino and his family. She only knew she was in love with him, and surely, from everything Gino had said and done all summer, he was in love with her?

Jane was still awake, lying head propped up on her arms, on the bed, when Meg came in.

'Oh, what a shame, Gino not turning up. You missed a super evening—I felt quite tearful about going back to England. Wished I was staying on like you.' She threw her cardigan on the bed and smiled round at Jane. 'Well, almost. Except that Tony's waiting for me. I know—we'll come to Rome for our honeymoon. Perhaps you'll be still here. Perhaps with Gino?'

'Oh, I don't know.' Jane looked away, feeling an uncertainty that had not been there until Vance Morley had put doubts in her mind. 'We—nothing is—is definite.'

'Have you been here all evening, then?' Meg asked to change the subject, as she began to undress.

'No. I—I had coffee with that man—you know, the one I told you about—who interrupted me the other evening.'

'How did you meet *him* again?' and Jane proceeded to tell Meg of her evening's encounter.

The next day Jane went with Meg and Bill and Tina to the airport to see them off. Tina was flying to Zürich to stay with friends before her winter sports job started, while the other two were returning to England. It was a melancholy morning, not helped by the fact that there was still no message from Gino.

If I don't hear from him today, Jane decided, sitting on the bus that took her back into Rome, I shall spend the afternoon checking on some of these addresses for rooms and flats.

She tidied up the room, in chaos after Meg's departure, and washed out tights and undies and then made coffee and a sandwich. The streets below were quieter—in October the noise and the traffic lessened, but there was still a cacophony of sound from cars and buses and mopeds. She waited for a while to allow prospective landlords to finish their siesta and then, gathering up the cuttings from advertisements, clicked the door of the flat shut after her and went out.

Halfway down the many flights of stairs she heard the footsteps of someone coming up them, and looking over the iron railing she saw a crisp brown head, and the next moment the smiling upturned face of Gino.

He waved and started to run up the stairs towards her. She ran down and they met on the bend.

'Jane, *cara mia*, what must you think of me? I cannot apologise too much for last night. I am sorry—sorry—sorry,' and his arms came about her and he bent his handsome head to kiss her.'

'Oh, Gino!' It was a sigh of relief, of happiness. For a moment they stood, arms about one another, then Gino, keeping one arm about her waist, turned her towards the stairs again and said,

'Did you wait long at the Toscano? I had intended to telephone a message to you there—someone would surely have found you—but I was delayed and by the time I could do so I knew that you would have gone.' He smiled penitently round at her. 'Perhaps gone away very angry with Gino—perhaps saying you would never speak with him again.'

She shook her head.

'I realised that something important must have come up. I thought perhaps your family had come back later than expected and you'd been held up?' She did not add that she had been at the Toscano all evening—she would explain that to Gino later.

He nodded vigorously.

'It was exactly so. A—a family—how do you say—complication. Nothing to worry about—it is settled. Now tell me—you have obtained the position with Enrico Baldoni?'

'Yes. Isn't it super? I start in a week's time.'

They had reached the ground floor, passed through the dark doorway into the street beyond, where, parked against the pavement, Jane could see Gino's car, a cream Mercedes.

He gestured.

'I thought we would go somewhere for a drink. And then I have a small surprise. That is——' He hesitated, looking round at her. 'Tell me first—you have not found the new *appartamento*?'

She shook her head.

'Not yet. I'm still looking.'

He smiled, holding open the car door for her so that she could slide into the front seat.

'We will find it together.'

Gino concentrated on driving through the whirling maelstrom that was Roman traffic; a succession of cars which drove full-tilt into one only to avert a collision at the last possible moment. A momentary hold-up brought on a blare of merciless hooting, then they were away again, weaving their way past the iced-cake splendour of the Vittorio Emmanuele monument, past the Forum lying below the level of the road, its green sprinkled with sightseers, its monuments seats for tourists. Here was the Palatine and then the massive ruin of the Colosseum. Jane always felt a thrill at seeing it—remembering the awe with which she had first viewed it, seeing the great amphitheatre which had once held fifty thousand spectators, imagining the roar and thunder of voices when the gladiators had fought with wild beasts and with one another. Today it was a silent haunted place, peopled only by sightseers and the dozens of thin little cats which ran about its corridors and underground chambers.

There were so many Romes, Jane thought. Imperial Rome, mightiest of all, perhaps. Then medieval Rome with its great churches and towers. Rome of the Renaissance when the great Basilica of St. Peter had been conceived and which, so it was said, could contain the entire cathedral of Milan. Baroque Rome, when the magnificent colonnade of St. Peter's Square had been designed and executed by Bernini, and the beautiful piazzas and fountains which gave Rome its inestimable grace had come into being. And lastly, eighteenth-century Rome which brought little change from the earlier majestic architecture, and so into modern Rome.

'Of what are you thinking?' Gino demanded with a turn of his head as the car swung on to an emptier road.

'I was thinking there is no city in the world like Rome and how little I really know about it. It has half a dozen cities and civilisations in one.'

'That is true.' Gino nodded proudly. 'A Roman feels he is different from any other man. It is a special feeling, I think. Now you are to stay in Rome you will learn much much more about it.'

'Yes, I want to do that.'

Gino had driven up into the hills beyond Rome and now he stopped the car outside a small restaurant set among trees. The garden was old-world with statuary, and flower-filled pots on a paved terrace and formal clipped hedges and a massive date palm rising out of a sea of hydrangeas. The leaves of the poplars shimmered in the sun. Some had already fallen to lie like golden coins on the grass. Jane had a sense of sadness, as if the falling leaves were an omen that the summer was over.

They ordered a pasta and some wine and when the waiter had gone Gino sighed and said,

'Ah, Jane, it is so good to be with you—to be at peace.' He shook his head. 'It is difficult with my family to be so—always there is much talk, many questions; always this affair and that affair to be discussed and arranged. You do not know what it has been like these past few days.'

'I thought Italians were easy-going and didn't worry.'

He shrugged.

'Not my family, believe me.'

'You've told me so little about your family.' Jane hesitated. 'Is it your—your—brother who tries to run things?'

Gino rolled his eyes.

'Oh, my brother and my mother and my uncle Pietro and my cousin Nicola and my aunt Teresa and'—he paused frowningly—'and my uncle Emilio. They would arrange my entire life for me if they could.'

'That does sound rather drastic.'

'Drastic? I do not know this word.'

'It means—well, sort of extreme.'

'Ah—*estremita*—yes, I understand. My family, they are so. But we have not come here to talk of them, Jane. We have come to be with ourselves, to talk together and to laugh. And later, I shall take you in my arms and kiss you and tell you that I love you. Do not blush and turn your head away, *cara mia*. You know how I feel about you.'

For a moment Jane didn't answer. She stared past Gino's curly head towards distant blue mountains. For some reason Vance Morley's words seems to echo in her mind and she wanted to turn to Gino and say, 'Please, I should so like to meet your family,' but she couldn't bring herself to do so, only feel angry for doubting Gino. Signora Abetti had only just returned to Rome, hadn't she? There was plenty of time ahead for Gino to arrange a meeting with his mother and Jane, or perhaps with his sister? Why should she worry about this or allow Vance Morley's casual remarks to shadow her meeting with Gino?

'Now you are *pensierosa*,' Gino said. 'You must drink more wine and then you will smile at me. Have I told you that your eyes are very beautiful? They are not grey nor brown, but something of both colour I think. When you are *pensierosa* as now they are dark and velvety, but when you are gay—suddenly they are bright and shining.' He looked across the table at her. 'You are wearing a new dress.'

'Not really. Perhaps you just haven't seen it before.'

Gino nodded approvingly. 'It is nice. Very nice. It goes with your hair, the same brown that is the colour of a thrush's wing, I think.'

Jane smiled.

'Thank you for the compliment. People usually call my hair mouse brown. Thrush colour sounds much better.'

It was sunset when they drove back to the city. The clouds were pink and peach-coloured, a thin sliver of a moon hung in the sky. In the Porto del Popolo the waters of the fountains cascaded in showers of gold against the blue night. Statues and domes, pillars and temples, churches and campaniles rose about the skyline, the static poetry that was Rome.

Gino drove along the Via dei Coronari and then turned right again and stopped in front of a handsome stucco-fronted house. He turned off the ignition and leaned back in his seat, saying with a flourish of one hand, 'See! We have arrived at your new apartment.'

Jane stared, looking at the wrought iron gates leading to a shadow-filled courtyard. A lamp gleamed down on a fountain, a statue and some greenery. She said somewhat hesisatingly,

'Really? It looks—very elegant.' She nearly added, 'And very expensive.'

'You like it?' Gino smiled. He slid out of his seat and came round to open the door for her. 'It is small inside but nice, I think. Come,' and he led the way into the courtyard towards a double doorway ornamented by heavy carving. At one end of the tiled foyer was a small lift and in a few seconds Jane was soaring upwards to what she saw would be the sixth floor. When the lift stopped Gino pushed open the door and they stepped out on to a narrow passageway. He went towards the door facing them and put a key in the lock and turned, smilingly.

'Please—this way.'

Jane walked through a minute hallway into the living-room and then halted with a gasp of astonishment.

The room was vast—it was obviously two thrown into one. A deeply piled olive-green carpet filled most of the polished wood floor, an enormous sofa, piled with cushions and covered with green and white mattress ticking, did duty as a bed. Two chairs to match faced it, with a most unusual coffee table, its sides opulently carved into a frieze of heads and flowers standing between. Above this hung a curving silver chandelier fitted with tall white candles. Bookshelves lined one wall, between two long windows, while a startlingly modern painting by Riopelle flooded colour on to another. The fourth wall was taken up by a louvred screen which, upon inspection, Jane discovered, hid a tiny kitchen and small separate loo and shower room.

She turned back into the living-room.

'I can't believe it! It isn't *really* for rent, is it? It must be fearfully expensive.'

Gino smiled.

'It is for you to live in, if you wish.' He walked over towards one long window and slid back a glass door. 'See.'

Jane stepped out on to a small roof terrace. Gino had switched on a lamp and she could see flower-filled pots and urns shining under it, and greenery entwining posts and pillars with beyond these, incredibly, one small spindly tree.

Beyond and below the terrace glittered the lights of Rome, the moving pinpoints of cars, the long avenues and lamplit piazzas. Across the gleaming waters of the river shone the Trastevere, its trees and bell towers outlined against the last flare of sunset.

She gasped with involuntary pleasure.

'It's *beautiful*! Beautiful and incredible. But who lives here—who does it belong to? Who could possibly want to rent such a place to a stranger?'

Gino came closer to her. He reached for her hand and raised it to his lips. Pressing a gentle kiss into the palm, he lifted his head and said slowly,

'Today it belongs to me, Jane. It is *my* flat. But now it is for you to live in—this winter in Rome.'

CHAPTER THREE

JANE stared at him.

'Yours? But I—I thought you lived somewhere off the Appian Way.'

Gino shrugged.

'Yes, at times. But that is my mother's house. It is not—not of convenience to be there always. This apartment belongs to a friend of mine—sometimes I share it with him. Now he is gone to the United States for some months and he has allowed me the use of it—to do as I wish.' He smiled at her, his golden brown eyes warm with light. 'It is your home now.'

'But I couldn't possibly,' Jane started to say. 'I mean, you—you must want it for yourself.'

He shook his head.

'No, it is for you to live here. It will be the answer of all your problems.'

Jane could feel herself frowning. She said determinedly, because some shadow of doubt was already coming up on the horizon,

'What—what would the rent be? We must—must make it a business arrangement.'

'There is no rent to pay, and it is not a business arrangement.' Gino answered. He reached out and pulled her close into his arms and she felt his mouth press against her hair. 'Don't you understand? Ah, Jane, we could be so happy here together.'

For a moment she stood there, aware only of the happiness of being near to Gino. Then some remnant of common sense jerked her back to practical realities and she said shakily, 'Together?'

Gino released her a fraction, to stare down at her with his shining brown eyes.

'Would it be so impossible, *cara*? That I should come here sometimes and be with you? I love you. You enchant me, Jane. I have never met a girl like you—so sweet, of such companionship. Is it not true that you have stayed here in Rome for my sake? It is inevitable that we should be together, always.'

Jane pulled herself free. She didn't know how to put her thoughts into words without making herself look foolish. 'Together always.' It sounded perfect, all that she desired. But in what context did Gino mean the phrase?

She bit her lip and said, uncertainly,

'I—I did stay in Rome to be near you, yes. I thought—I mean, I thought——' Her voice trailed off, wondering what exactly she had thought. That Gino would ask her to marry him? She took a deep breath and said slowly, 'I stayed on in Rome because I thought—I hoped that by so doing we would get to know one another better.'

Gino caught hold of her hand.

'But of course, *cara*. *Certamente*. That is exactly what we shall do—learn to know one another very very well.'

'Yes, but——' She was in deep waters again. 'Not by—by sharing your—this flat. I thought—perhaps I would meet your family.'

Gino dropped her hand abruptly. His handsome face darkened to a frown, his full lips set more firmly than usual. He shook his head.

'That would not be possible, Jane. Not at—at this time.'

There was a long pause. From somewhere in the street below a car exhaust exploded with a sudden noise. Someone shouted; the thin sound of music from a radio or T.V. set drifted up, a woman's voice singing one of the evocatively romantic songs that Italian music abounds in. Then Jane said slowly, painfully,

'Please tell me what you mean?'

Gino turned and took a pace to the window, turned again and paced back towards her. He stood irresolute, banging the fist of one hand against the palm of his other. He said jerkily,

'It—there is a family complication. It is not to do with me—I mean, not of my doing. You understand? It is a—an arrangement made without my consent—when I am young, before I am old enough to speak for myself, say what I wish.' He broke off, looking with pleading brown eyes at Jane. 'You will not understand if I tell you. You will turn against me—you will hate me and go away.'

Jane felt as if icicles were forming round her heart. She thought she already knew what he was going to tell her even as she said, as calmly as she could,

'I promise to try and understand if you will just be honest with me.'

Gino gazed at her, his face set, his eyes no longer sparkling, but shadowed and unhappy.

'Ah, Jane, I cannot bear it, that we should speak like this. All these questions, they are turning us into two strangers. This thing, it is nothing. It does not concern my regard for you. I could not love you less because of—of——' He broke off as if too unhappy to go on.

She finished the sentence for him, saying in a trembling voice,

'Because of some—some other girl?'

His face flushed beneath the smoothly golden tan. He sighed heavily.

'Yes. This—complication is made by my parents—by my father, when he is alive, that I am to marry one day with a cousin.' He frowned, shaking his head. 'A cousin of a cousin—a girl I scarcely know. Until this summer I had not met her for five, six years. Her family had been living in South America, now they have returned to Italy. When I am at Forte de Marmi—she is there staying, my sister-in-law has invited her. I talk with her, we swim—play tennis, but I am not—I *cannot* be in love with her. My heart belongs only to Jane.' He came towards her and caught hold of her hand.

'Believe me, *cara mia*, it is you I love. There can be no one else.'

Jane looked at him. She longed to move closer. She longed to throw her arms round Gino's neck and smooth the frown from his handsome face. His eyes were unhappy, luminous, as if with tears. That didn't surprise her. She knew that Italian men cried almost as easily as women. But it made her doubly unhappy to see how upset Gino was.

'Do—do your family still think you will—will marry your cousin?'

He bit his lip.

'I have tried to tell them, to explain my feelings to them, but my mother, she is old-fashioned and, since the death of my father, something of an autocrat. She will not listen. She insists that the arrangement will stand—that it is made in honour.' He tightened his grip on her fingers. 'Do not look like that, Jane, my darling. It will come right—I shall not be affianced to Francesca when it is you whom I love.'

Jane said slowly, almost despairingly,

'But you *are* affianced—until you tell your family otherwise. Your—your family will have to know about me, or—or the arrangement continues, I suppose.' She felt empty, drained, as if she could no longer cope with the situation. 'Does—is your cousin fond of you?'

Gino shrugged.

'It appears so. She is very young—eighteen years old only.'

'Does she live in Rome?'

He shook his head.

'No. In Florence. But—at present—this is the difficult situation—I did not know but when my mother returned to Rome on Friday, Francesca came with her, for a short visit. There was a family dinner party last evening—that is why I was unable to meet you.'

Jane was suddenly aware of how insuperable the whole situation was, how involved.

'I'm sorry,' she said, her voice not quite steady. 'It isn't

35

easy for you, Gino. I do understand. I just wish you'd said something about all this before.'

He gazed at her in astonishment.

'But if I had done perhaps you would not have come out with me. We would not have become known to one another.'

'No.' She turned away and picked up her shoulder bag. 'I—I think I should like to leave now. Don't bother to come with me—I can take a taxi back to the apartment.' She looked round at him. 'Of course, you know there's no question of my staying here—with or without you.'

He flung his hands out.

'But, *cara*, why? Why cannot you? It is for you, as I have said. No rent.' He attempted a smile. 'No complication. I will stay away and never come—except by invitation. It will be for you to use as you wish.'

Jane shook her head.

'I'd rather not. And if—your cousin is here in Rome, staying with your family, perhaps it would be better if we didn't meet. For the present, anyway.'

'Jane—*please*.' He caught both her hands in his, pressed quick kisses on to them. 'Please, *cara mia*. Why must you go?' His hands slid up her arms,, he pulled her close against him. 'My sweet Jane, do not leave me. We could be happy —so happy. Francesca means nothing to me—I will tell my mother, my brother, my uncle, I will not marry someone whom I do not love.'

She managed to resist him, to pull herself free, though she was shaking all over with the effort of it all.

'I can't stay. I must go, Gino.'

His face darkened as she moved towards the door.

'You are so prim. Prim and English. But not all English girls are as you are!' He flung the words after her in anger.

Jane didn't answer. She had just enough self-control left to open the door of the tiny hall and stumble towards the lift. As the door slid to she heard Gino's voice calling from the corridor, but she couldn't make out the words. The lift slid downwards and in a few moments she was out of the building and into the street. Along the main thoroughfare there were lights and cars and cruising taxis. She managed to hail one and fell into the back seat, murmuring the address to the driver. She sat hunched up, shivering but dry-eyed, and she was back in the cold little apartment she had shared with Meg before she started to cry.

She couldn't stop. It was like the end of a marvellous dream. She was so in love with Gino and now she learned he had a fiancée. Even if, as he had assured her, he wasn't in love with this girl. Jane believed him. But she knew enough by now of the close complex of Italian family life to realise that he might not be able to break the association so easily as he hoped. If he did hope? Yes, of course he did. But——

But she couldn't possibly stay in his flat. That was one thing. Then there was this new job she was supposed to be starting. That was another. It might lead to all sorts of complications. Jane couldn't easily forget the curious way Signor Baldoni had regarded her, the odd questions he had asked her about Gino; how well she knew him, how long they had been friends. It had all seemed unnecessarily personal.

She scarcely slept that night. Next day Sunday was a long blank spell of time to be got through. She spent it re-reading the advertisements for rooms and apartments to let. She wrote a letter to Rosemary, telling her she expected to be moving from the flat and would send a new address as soon as she had one.

As well as feeling deeply unhappy she was lonely and it dawned on Jane for the first time how much she had depended on her job at the Agency for personal contacts and friendship and how Gino had taken up the rest of her time. What would life be like in Rome without Meg and the other girls, and, most of all, without Gino? She was utterly depressed by the thought.

Monday morning came thankfully and soon after Jane's breakfast of half a roll and hot black coffee, an enormous bouquet of roses arrived with a note attached, 'Forgive me. I will come and see you today. All my love, Gino.'

The heady scent filled the bleak room, sparser than ever now Meg's colourful clutter had been removed. Jane hovered over the flowers, touching the rich red petals, closing her eyes to breathe in the perfume and longing for Gino to come, yet dreading his arrival.

When he finally appeared it was all she could do to stop herself rushing into his arms. She opened the door at his ring and there he stood, handsome head slightly on one side, golden brown eyes warm and pleading, both hands outstretched towards her.

'Jane, sweet wonderful Jane!' he said caressingly. 'Jane, I have been distracted, desperate. I have not eaten or slept since last we met. Jane, we must not be apart. I cannot bear it.'

'Oh, Gino!' was all she could say in answer.

He caught her round the waist as she turned back into the room. 'I am forgiven? Please kiss me, Jane, so that I shall know it is so.'

She submitted to his close embrace, to the ardent kiss which before she would have responded to. Then she managed to free herself and move away, steadying her voice to say,

'Th-thank you for the lovely roses.'

'It is nothing. The smallest expression of my feelings for you. Are you ready? I have come to take you out to luncheon.'

'But I wasn't expecting—I'm not ready——'

Gino waved an expressive hand.

'Five minutes—ten. I will wait.' He glanced round, 'This place, it is not good. You would be much happier in *my* apartment.'

Jane didn't answer but hurried away to comb her hair and put on fresh lipstick. A few moments later they were driving along the Via del Corso towards another of their favourite restaurants. Despite her happiness at being with

Gino again, she felt awkward, less than herself. She wanted to ask questions; she wanted to know if he had spent all yesterday with his cousin, she wanted to know when Francesca was going back to Florence. But, of course, she had only just arrived.

Gino sensed her reserve, for he reached across the table to clasp her fingers.

'What is wrong, Jane? You are not still angry with me?'

'No, of course not. It—it isn't your fault—about your cousin, I mean. But—but it does make a difference. Things can't be the same for us.'

He frowned.

'Why should that not be? I am still in love with you, and Francesca will be gone in a few days.'

'Yes, but—but you're supposed to be *engaged* to her, whether she's here or in Florence. Don't you understand? In the circumstances, until things are—are changed—we can't go on as before.'

'But I do not love her. I have told you so.'

'That's beside the point. It's a—a question of facing up to the—the situation and being honest with your—your family and—and Francesca.'

Gino stared blankly at Jane as if he wondered what she was talking about. Then he shrugged.

'You are jealous of Francesca—there is no need.'

He was so outrageous she almost laughed. Instead Jane heard herself saying, uncertainly,

'Will you tell your family about us?'

His two hands came up in the air.

'I—could not do so at this moment. My mother has not good health—she would be made ill. My uncle, who is head of the business since my father has died, would be angry. He has much—what do you say? *ponteza*—power. It would not be—wise. You understand my difficulty, Jane?'

She understood all too well.

'Yes.'

Afterwards Jane wondered how she got through the rest

of the meal; it was as much as she could do to swallow the usually delicious *abbacchio* down. She refused the array of tempting sweets and settled for coffee. Only the wine, red and warming, seemed to revive her so that somehow she was able to go on talking to Gino, smiling at remarks the sense of which she scarcely registered. But at last it was over and Gino was saying something about going back to his apartment before returning to the office.

'Will you come with me? Please, *cara*.'

Light-headed, a trifle dazed, Jane was still rational enough to refuse his request and mumble something about an appointment.

'Then I will take you to wherever you must go. If it is so important,' Gino added reproachfully.

'Thank you, but I—I would rather walk. I feel—it was very stuffy in the restaurant.'

Gino took her arm.

'You are well? You look pale, *cara mia*.'

'I'm fine,' Jane assured him.

'Tomorrow we shall have dinner together? I am not—not free tonight, that is why I came at *mezzogiorno*.'

The sun was hot on their heads. It made Jane feel dizzy. She took a deep breath and said as calmly as she could,

'I understand. Thank you for the super lunch, Gino. I must go now.'

'Of course. *Arrivederci*, Jane.' His lips brushed hers and with a graceful wave of the hand he turned towards his parked car.

Jane walked in the opposite direction on legs that felt distinctly peculiar. She crossed into the shade of the street. She would be all right in a few moments. She walked along the Via Ludovisi and into another wider street. She gazed around, wondering where she was, her brain hardly functioning. She turned left and walked on a little further and then saw, with a click of recognition, that she had reached the Via Sistina, and that to the right were the twin towers of Santa Trinita dei Monti and the curving splendour of the Spanish Steps.

When she finally arrived there she plodded up the first dozen or so and then flopped down on the shady side of them. She closed her eyes and rested her head against the cool stonework, wishing she had not drunk so much wine after so meagre a breakfast.

And as Jane sat there, exhausted and unhappy, she wished fervently that she had never decided to stay on in Rome. There was no future in it. She could see now that Gino was too enmeshed in his family, too dependent upon his mother and his uncle and the older members to make any gestures of defiance over his engagement to Francesca. At least, at this stage. What then, she wondered tiredly, did he intend to do?

Nothing very much, perhaps. If Jane remained in Rome they could be together whenever Gino was free of family commitments. Through his influence with Enrico Baldoni Jane had found a job. But she had to remember that all the staff were Italians. It wouldn't be like working with Meg and the others. Nor would she have the companionship of the holidaymakers she had met while working with the Dana Tourist Agency.

She opened her eyes and stared unseeingly at the procession of people drifting up and down the steps; tourists and sightseers, priest and hippies and black-clad elderly women. Americans and Germans and French and Dutch and Indians and Japanese; a collection of people of all ages and all nations, a melting pot of colour and fashion and creed.

If she stayed on in Rome she was going to be unutterably lonely at times. Why hadn't she thought of that before?

Because all she had done was picture herself with Gino, imagining herself becoming part of an Italian family, welcomed into their circle, meeting their friends.

That couldn't happen now. Because of Francesca. Whether Gino loved her or not didn't matter. She was part of his family's plans for him and because of this fact Jane would not be wanted.

41

She knew the danger of remaining in Rome near Gino; realising how involved she might become because of her isolation and possible loneliness, because she was so much in love with him.

Then what should she do? Go back to England? She couldn't bear the idea, it seemed such an admittance of failure, an anticlimax to all the plans she had made. She closed her eyes again as if to shut out the problem. Her head was aching dully. She thought that in a few minutes she would make an effort and go down to the Babington Tea Rooms at the foot of the steps.

She sensed, rather than saw someone drop down beside her, heard the scrape of shoes on the stone, the movement of legs and arms. Then a voice said,

'I thought only mad dogs and Englishmen went out in the midday sun, but it seems there are plenty of other crazy people around.'

Against her will Jane's heavy eyelids opened. She turned her head and saw Vance Morley squatting on the step beside her, hands linked loosely between jack-knifed knees, a lock of black hair falling across his frowning forehead.

She couldn't think of anything more to say than, 'Oh.'

'I'm sorry if I startled you. I sat down as quietly as I could. I knew you weren't asleep because I saw you before, as I walked up to the Piazza Trinita. You were staring into space. I waved to you, but you didn't seem to see me.'

'No.'

He stared at her, his grey eyes narrowing.

'I can see you're in no mood to be chatted up. Nothing wrong, is there?'

'No. Why should there be?'

He shrugged.

'I don't know. I thought you looked melancholy sitting here.'

Jane said flatly,

'I had too much wine with my lunch. It made me feel dopey, that's all.'

He stared gravely at her.

'Ah. Your Italian friend.' It was a statement rather than a question and Jane ignored it. They sat in silence, staring at the scene below; the Piazza di Spagna filled with people and moving traffic, the Fontana della Barcaccia playing in the afternoon sunlight, the flower stalls rioting with colour. Jane wished Vance would go away and leave her alone. She couldn't forgive him for warning her about the dangers of her friendship with Gino; of being proved right so that if he had but known he would say, 'I told you so.'

As if reading her thoughts, he said,

'I'm leaving tomorrow. Going on to Corfu, as I said.'

'Oh.' She was faintly interested. 'You've stopped marking time?'

'Not quite. I'm in no hurry to get there. I shall drive the long way round, through the mountains. I might stop a couple of nights in Naples—Capri's lovely at this time of the year.'

She said idly,

'I've a friend living in Naples, a girl who used to work at the Dana Agency. She married an American who is now attached to the Zoological Station there.'

'Interesting. Have you been to Naples?'

'No. I shall go some time. Diana, my friend, has invited me to stay whenever I like.'

He lifted a black eyebrow.

'I can drop you off there, on my way. You're between jobs, aren't you? Plenty of time to "see Naples and die" before next Monday.' He turned to look at her. 'How about it?'

He had put into words the glimmer of an idea that had come to Jane while they were talking. She said lightly,

'I might take you up on that.'

'You'll have to make your mind up quickly. I'm leaving first thing in the morning.'

Faced with a sudden decision, she stalled.

'Oh, I—couldn't go as suddenly as that. I—I have to

43

make arrangements.'

'With the Italian job? You never know—absence might make the heart grow fonder. Though I must say he seems devoted enough.'

Jane didn't answer. She was thinking about the flat. The rent was paid to the end of the month and notice to quit had already been given. She could store a suitcase with the *portinaia* and travel light to Naples. Diana might help her to find a job.

But I can't go away, she thought. I can't leave Rome—and Gino.

Vance Morley saw the indecision in her face, for he said abruptly, rising to his feet,

'I'm going to change some travellers' cheques. If you're free this evening would you like to meet me for a drink? You can tell me then what you're going to do. If you want to come along we can make the necessary arrangements. If you decide to stay on here, we can share a farewell drink. That suit?'

She nodded, not wanting to commit herself.

'Yes. Thank you.'

'Right.' He turned and then half turned back. 'Better still, make it dinner. Do you know Marion's? It's in the Via delle Vite. About nine?' He lifted a casual hand. 'See you.'

Jane watched him saunter down the steps, outstandingly tall, his well-shaped head oddly graceful above the breadth of shoulder. Two pretty girls coming up the steps turned to look round at him, but he didn't appear to notice them. Jane supposed they thought he was attractive. He was, but she wasn't interested. All her thoughts were centred on Gino.

By nine o'clock she still hadn't made up her mind. She had cleared out drawers, packed a suitcase of things she could leave behind if she wanted to, and left another case empty, ready to fill if she decided to go to Naples. One thing she had made up her mind on; she would not take the job with the Baldoni firm.

To that effect Jane wrote a letter of apology to Signor Baldoni saying that owing to unforeseen circumstances she would not be able to start work at his offices on the following Monday as arranged. That made her feel slightly better. She could still remain in Rome if she wanted to, but might get something like an au pair job, live with a family rather than in lonely rooms on her own.

She changed her suede skirt and suede jerkin for a dress of red and green jersey. It was casual but gay. She brushed out her long brown hair and applied a brighter lipstick so as to give colour to her unusually pale face. Then she set off to meet Vance Morley.

He was waiting for her, looking unexpectedly well groomed in a smooth tweed jacket over dark trews. To date she hadn't seen him in anything but casual sweaters and khaki drills.

'Hello.' He didn't smile, and for the first time it struck her that he was an oddly unsmiling sort of man.

'Have you made up your mind yet?' he asked, as they sat down at the table reserved for them.

Jane shook her head.

'N-not really. I'm still at the dithering stage.'

'Waiting to have it made up for you, perhaps?'

'Perhaps.'

He put his head on one side to consider her.

'You hardly strike me as being a girl who doesn't know her own mind. Although you're small and—very feminine-looking, I imagine you can be decided enough if you want to be.'

'Possibly—sometimes.'

Vance Morley ordered the meal—soup and then *saltim-bocca* and a Verdicchio to drink with it. Conversation was desultory. Jane was quietly depressed over Gino and Vance seemed preoccupied, as if he too had problems on his mind. She couldn't help wondering why he had asked her to have dinner with him, why indeed he had suggested giving her a lift in his car as far as Naples. He didn't appear to need

45

company and certainly he had little personal interest in her.

When dinner was over and they came out into the warm blue night, Vance looked down at her and said,

'We don't seem to have come to any conclusions. Would you like to walk round for a bit?'

'Yes, that would be nice.'

They strolled along the street and turned right, crossing into the wide Via delle Tritone and then turning right again, came out by the Trevi fountain. As usual people were clustered around it, staring admiringly or sitting on the wall close by. As usual it looked even more magnificent by night than by day, the columns and statues rising nobly above the rugged rocks and leaping horses. The waters shone golden under the lights, while on the marble below the coins shimmered dully.

'Did you throw yours in?' Vance asked.

'Almost my first day here. To make sure I should return to Rome.'

He smiled.

'It's a good gag. And steps up the funds for charity, I'm told.'

Jane sighed, staring about her.

'It's magical—like most of Rome.'

'But you must know all the famous sights backwards—as part of your job. Do you still feel the same first thrill?'

'Yes. I shall never grow tired of it.'

They turned and walked slowly on, pausing to look at Bernini's charming little Triton's fountain in the Piazza Barberini and eventually reaching the Via Vittorio Veneto.

Vance gestured.

'Shall we walk up and have a last drink at one of the plush hotels?'

'If you like, thank you.'

'And then you'll tell me what you're going to do?'

'Yes.' Jane almost said there and then, 'I expect it will be "No". I don't feel I want to leave Rome,' but still she hesitated. They walked along the crowded pavements,

46

pressed closely side by side by the throngs of people saunt-
ering past the terraces of the hotels and cafés. There was a
space outside the Excelsior—a commissionaire came out to
hail a taxi, while at the same moment a car drew up and a
group of people descended on to the pavement. Jane heard
laughter, the sound of voices and looking round, saw a tall
elegantly dressed woman with beautifully groomed grey
hair, a handsome middle-aged man, an attractive dark girl
in her late twenties walking towards the doors of the hotel,
while the fourth person, a man, helped out the last occupant
of the car.

The man said something in Italian as he took the arm of
a small slim girl. She looked up at him and smiled. She was
exquisitely pretty, with sleek dark hair lifting in a wide
sweep from a smooth forehead; she had winged dark eyebrows above sparkling black eyes, red lips and a creamy
skin. A coat of shocking pink silk was worn over a matching
dress, on tiny feet were gold wedge-heeled sandals. No
wonder the man gazed so attentively at her, so admiringly.

Jane was frozen into immobility where she stood. She
couldn't have moved even if she had wanted to. And she
didn't want to. She wanted to stay quite still and unnoticed
until the smiling couple on the pavement before he had
disappeared into the hotel.

Because the young man was Gino.

She felt Vance Morley's hand under her arm, his grip
tighten as if to steady her as the two figures moved, the
doors of the hotel swung behind them and Jane found herself being propelled forward.

They walked on in silence. Her thoughts were a whirling
mixture of jealousy and despair. So that was Francesca!
She was beautiful, and very young. And somehow—charming. The older woman must have been Gino's mother, the
older man his uncle. Or his brother? No, he would be too
old to be Gino's brother. The uncle. And the other girl?
His sister-in-law, perhaps.

How gay they had all looked—a happy family party out

for the evening, out to celebrate something?

She felt herself tremble and heard Vance Morley say,

'We'll stop here—it looks a good place.'

Jane sat down in the chair he pulled forward and pushed her loose hair back from her forehead. She wasn't hot, only curiously cold.

'What will you have to drink? Campari—Cinzano?' and when Jane stared blankly at him as if unable to speak he ordered two Cinzanos. She shook her head at the proffered cigarette. He took one for himself without speaking and then, after smoking in silence for a few minutes, he said briefly,

'That must have come as rather a shock.'

Jane came to with a jerk. The last thing in the world she wanted was for this dark stranger to be sorry for her, to be able to say 'I told you so.' She heard herself say jerkily, stammeringly,

'I—I knew about—Gino's fi-fiancée.'

The pewter-grey eyes narrowed. He said slowly, 'You *knew*?'

She lifted the glass to her lips and sipped the Cinzano. Despite the ice in it, the drink warmed her, revived her.

'Yes. He—he told me about her. It's one of those—those long-standing family things.'

Vance's expression didn't change. He looked remote, uninterested, as he stared over her head at the passers by.

'I see.'

She was too preoccupied with her own distraught emotions to pay attention to this indifferent manner. She finished the Cinzano off in one gulp and said hurriedly, before she had a chance to change her mind,

'By the way, I—I've decided. If the offer still holds I'd like to—to go with you as far as Naples.'

CHAPTER FOUR

JANE had caught him off guard. He turned his head to stare blankly at her. For one moment she thought that he had forgotten that he'd ever invited her, yet only a little while ago they had discussed the possibility.

'Oh. Yes, all right.'

'You're sure? I mean, you haven't changed your mind about—about taking a passenger?'?

'No. No, of course not. You're welcome.'

He sounded so abrupt and offhand that Jane felt that suddenly he didn't want to take her and she wished she hadn't mentioned the idea. Yet Vance had asked her if she was waiting to have her mind made up for her and she'd answered 'Perhaps'. Well, it *had* been made up. Very definitely. Ever since she'd seen Gino with his family and Francesca. All she wanted now was to get away from Rome as soon as she could.

Vance Morley signalled to the waiter.

'I expect you've things to arrange. We'd better go. What time can you be ready in the morning?'

'Whenever you want me to be. I haven't much to pack. I shall have to see the *portinaia* before I leave, to give her the key of the apartment and if possible, I'd like to cash a cheque.'

'I'll collect you at ten o'clock.' He stood up, a tall dark man, staring down at her with an expression at once sombre and forbidding. 'Come on, we'll take a taxi.'

He dropped Jane off at her flat and said shortly,

'See you in the morning.'

'Yes. I'll be ready.' She looked up at him. 'Thank you for—for dinner and everything. Goodnight.'

'Goodnight.' His voice was as aloof as his glance. When he turned away she felt a sinking of heart and wondered how uncomfortable a journey they were likely to share. But there was no time to worry about that; at the most it would only be for a few hours. Meanwhile she had dozens of things to attend to before she could hope to sleep.

She was glad to be busy. It took her mind off Gino and the thought of leaving him. Writing the note she was to leave for him was the hardest thing she had to do. After several abortive efforts she made it as brief as possible, and wrote simply,

'Dear Gino, I have thought things over and decided to leave Rome for the time being. I don't think you will be able to alter things with your family. If I stay here we may both be unhappy. Thank you for the wonderful summer we shared.' She signed it 'Jane' without further embellishment.

She felt more sad than she could say; there was something final about closing the door on the apartment she had shared with Meg and going away from Rome without even saying goodbye to Gino. She wanted to persuade herself that she could stay, that everything would turn out right in the end but she knew that was a dangerous weakness. Seeing Gino with his family this evening, seeing that devastatingly pretty girl with her expensive clothes and air of luxury had made Jane very conscious of being an outsider, someone foreign to another way of life. It would be difficult, if not impossible, for Gino to break away and Jane had been too involved with him to remain in Rome and aloof from his persuasions. If it was cowardly to run away it was also wise.

It was after one o'clock when she finally dropped into bed and, tired as she was, she found it impossible to sleep. It was early morning before she dozed off, and then it was only fitfully, for she was frightened of oversleeping and not being ready when Vance Morley called for her. When, yawning and gritty-eyed, she washed and dressed in readiness for him she was aware of looking plain and tired. Not that it mattered. Masochistically she caught her straggling brown hair back into a rubber band and pulled the suede jerkin over the black cotton sweater, trying not to remember how Gino had so often called her his 'beautiful Jane'.

She said goodbye to the wizened little *portinaia* and gave her the note for Gino and the suitcase to keep in custody, and then as a final gesture, a small roll of lire for herself. The old lady came after her, smiling and chattering, and there was Vance Morley's car parked by the pavement.

He lifted a hand in casual greeting and came to take the case from Jane, turning to say 'good morning' to the *portinaia*.

'Everything in order?' he asked as he closed the door on Jane.

She nodded. 'Yes. I've been to the bank—it was open at eight-thirty.'

'Good.'

As if to match Jane's melancholy mood, the weather had broken and it was raining. Rome lay under a drizzle as misty and grey as London, and she was glad; it was easier to leave it this way, with the traffic whirling noisily round, splashing the pedestrians, bent under their black umbrellas, dampening golden stone and creamy columns to dim ruins, muting the colour and the splendour of the city. On the balconies of the tall flats the trees were tossing their arms in the wind, grateful for the rain. Jane never ceased to marvel how such burgeoning gardens could exist so high above the city; rose trees and cypress, ilex and poplar, ivy and vine and trailing tradescantia clambering over the bleak iron railings, softening the harsh lines of the otherwise uncompromisingly functional buildings.

They were both silent as they drove along. Vance seemed preoccupied, perhaps concentrating on getting clear of Rome, or perhaps because such a mood was habitual to him, while Jane was closed up in her own world of heartache and regret.

For the first part of the journey the road ran close to the Rome–Naples autostrada and at one point the autostrada cut across it and the railway too was frequently within

51

sight. It was still raining when they left both rail and auto-strada to go through the Sacco valley and drive towards Ferentino.

'You're very quiet this morning,' Vance said suddenly.

Jane blinked, coming back to life.

'I was thinking the—the same thing of you.'

He shrugged.

'The fact is, we both have a problem.' She could feel his sideways glance at her. 'I take it you're running away from yours.'

'In a way, yes. Are you?'

He shook his head frowningly.

'I'm running towards mine. Slowly. I'm in no hurry to confront it.'

She wondered what the problem could be. Money? A job? Most likely a girl. She would have liked to ask, but something in his aloof dark face deterred her.

'Your problem will be waiting for you when you get back. The situation, I mean.' He shook his head again. 'It beats me how a girl as seemingly intelligent as you can be so stupid.'

She was too flabbergasted to say that she wasn't return-ing to Rome. She simply stared at him, taken aback by his frankness of speech.

'Stupid?'

'Well, of course.' His voice was impatient. 'It's the sort of thing every little teenage holidaymaker falls for—a good-looking Italian, some smooth talk, a few compliments. Eng-lish girls abroad make fools of themselves, but I should have thought you'd have known better. You've worked in the country, you speak the language—you must have a few clues.'

She found her voice at last.

'I think you're being very rude! And very s-sweeping in your s-statements.' She was stammering with protest. 'Every girl doesn't f-fall for some man when she comes abroad. That's ridiculous.'

52

'It's a fact. From the Costa Brava to the Greek Islands the young men are waiting to pounce upon the so-called swinging British female. They can't get to first base with their own countrywomen—not the single ones who are guarded and cherished by their wily relatives until marriage.'

If she could have stopped the car and got out and walked, even in the pouring rain, Jane would have done so. Instead all she could do was say vehemently,

'I think you're s-stupid too. Stupid and narrow and old-fashioned. Of course on holiday girls like to meet someone —have some sort of romance. Not necessarily with a—a foreigner. It might be an Englishman they meet abroad.'

'Let's get away from the general to the particular. You've come abroad to work and the first thing you've done is fall hook, line and sinker for a trendy young Italian. Who happens to have a fiancée. Rather a dishy one, too. The competition's likely to be formidable if we take Mama into consideration.'

She wanted to cry out, 'It isn't like that,' but the words wouldn't come. Because, under all the protestation and argument, the truth ran like a cold stream. It *was* like that. But she wasn't going to tell this hateful Vance Morley so. Or explain that she had said goodbye to Gino for good because she had come to her senses after learning about Francesca.

She said through gritted teeth,

'I wish I'd never accepted a lift from you. I think it's foul of you to get me in your car where I'm absolutely trapped and c-can't escape and then turn on me. What business is it of yours what I do or how I feel—what my personal problems are? Please sh-shut up and leave me alone!'

Now she was being as rude as he, but when he spoke his voice was calm and unruffled.

'As you say, your affairs are no business of mine. But when we were talking last night and you told me about looking after your mother and then being left on your own

53

and changing your job and coming to work out here, I admired your courage and independence. I thought also that you could be—what's the word—exposed to danger—vulnerable. In a way I was sorry for you.'

She exploded at that.

'Please don't be *sorry* for me! I couldn't bear that. I don't know you, I don't like you, and you're the last person in the world whose advice I would welcome. I wish you could drop me at the nearest railway station and I'll get the train the rest of the way to Naples.'

He said mildly,

'It's no use blowing your top. I'm just trying to help in a—let's call it an avuncular way. Instead of going to Naples for a week you ought to be catching the next plane back to England. If I had any sense I would see you did just that.'

'By what right do you constitute yourself my *keeper*?' Jane demanded angrily. 'I think you must be mad! We're practically strangers.'

'Because you're an innocent abroad and more crazy than I think you are if you return to Rome and that predatory boy-friend.'

They had driven through Ferentino in a babel of angry words, oblivious to its ancient buildings, great ramparts and massive walls; the Cathedral and the Bishop's Palace looming above them through the silvery rain. The town fell away behind them and they were on the open road again, the hills on either side rising up towards castellated villages.

Jane scarcely noticed anything; she was sitting hunched up in a corner as far away from Vance Morley as she could, staring out at the rain-drenched landscape with unseeing eyes.

Fortunately he provoked her no further, but drove on in an equally pregnant silence, and in a short time they reached Frosinone.

'I thought we'd stop here for something to eat,' Vance said.

'I'm not hungry, thank you.'

'Rubbish. Of course you want some food—and I most certainly could do with a drink. A strong one.' He parked the car near the small square and said, 'Over there looks a likely place.'

Jane wanted to remain in the car, nursing her resentment, but Vance held the door open in determined fashion and said,

'No use sitting there sulking. Come along.'

'I'm not *sulking*——' she began furiously, and then stopped. What was the use of talking to him—arguing? She would keep quiet—not speak unless absolutely necessary. In a few hours they would be at Naples.

The hotel was small and unpretentious, but the meal was excellent—that was, if one had the appetite to enjoy it. But even with Vance sitting across the table from her and passing condiments and bread and pouring wine with elaborate politeness, Jane found herself able to do justice to the food. Perhaps it was the unexpected cold, the chill of rain after the Indian summer weather that had made her hungry.

'Do you feel better now?' The grey eyes—dark, almost gunmetal colour—observed her more closely. 'You *look* better.'

'Thank you, yes.' Her voice was stiff. 'How—far are we from Naples?'

'About ninety miles, perhaps more. You'll have to put up with me for a bit longer.'

She refused to be provoked. She would maintain a front of courtesy and good manners.

'I just wondered.'

He glanced at the dark sky beyond the shuttered windows.

'Pity it's raining—it's quite a pleasant run in the ordinary way. We go through Cassino, where there was such bloody fighting in the last war. An uncle of mine, my father's brother, was killed at Cassino—he's buried in the British Military Cemetery there—the largest one in Italy.

God knows how many died in that battle—until finally a Polish Division captured the San' Angelo ridge and two days later the Polodski Lancers hoisted the Polish standard above the ruins.'

'You know a lot about it.'

'My father fought there too—but he came home safely. He used to tell me about it when I was a boy.'

It was too wet to walk in the town, so they went back to the car to resume the journey. They came to a village and crossed a swiftly running stream.

'The Liri,' Vance said in his laconic way. 'It runs into the Garigliano further down. This valley—the Liri valley —was all part of the assault on Monte Cassino.'

Silence fell again as they drove on. Jane, gazing out of the window, saw the sky clearing above a small castle set on the hillside. A few miles further on Vance gestured towards another village lying below the road on the right-hand side.

'Aquino. It was quite a town in Roman days—Aquinum. The ruins extend a long way over there. Keep your eyes open—you'll see a place called Monte Cairo in a few minutes—part of the defence lines of the Germans in 1943.'

Jane stared up at the bare forbidding bastion as it came into sight and then Vance said,

'There's Monte Cassino—with the town below.'

The hill before them rose above the town, which looked new with its modern buildings and wide streets.

Vance stopped the car and they both stared up at the mountain and the Abbey with all its associations of bitter war.

'Can you visit the Abbey?' Jane asked.

'Yes. You have to walk—it's quite a climb.' He looked at the wet road. 'Hardly the day for that, but there are fantastic views from the ascent. I've been myself and into the church, which has been rebuilt, of course. Would you like to chance it?'

She shook her head quickly.

56

'No—no, thank you.'

'Just as well—it takes half a day—you wouldn't be in Naples until late evening. What time is our friend expecting you?'

'I wasn't able to contact her—I tried to telephone last night, but there was no reply—and I hadn't time this morning. It doesn't matter—if she isn't there I'll find somewhere to stay.'

He turned his head to stare frowningly at her.

'But you've never been to Naples before—you don't know the first thing about the place.'

'I can find a hotel.'

'Look,' he had turned off the road a few minutes before and now he stopped the car, 'I'm not having the responsibility of leaving you in a city like Naples unless I know you're safely looked after. Your friend had *better* be at home when I dump you there.'

Jane looked at him coldly.

'Or else? What do you think you're going to do about it? You're being quite absurd. I speak fluent Italian—I happen to be trained as a *courier*, someone capable of seeing other people from A. to B. I look after *them*. Don't you think I can look after myself—book myself into a hotel if necessary? Find my way around.'

'Quite frankly, no. I think you're guileless and immature. If you weren't you'd never have got yourself involved with the first young Italian who tried to make you.'

She said furiously, all her resolutions to remain calm and detached, flying to the four winds,

'Why don't you leave Gino out of this discussion?'

'Because your romantic attachment to him shows the kind of girl you are. The impressionable, gullible type. You told me yourself this—this Gino had a long-standing family arrangement with the girl you saw him with last night. Did you think he was going to break it for you?' He shook his head. 'Not a hope. He just hoped to have you too, on the side. Because don't tell me he *didn't* try to make you.'

She opened her mouth in angry protest, and then the memory of the visit to Gino's flat came back to her and all the hidden implication of his offer for her to live there, and she was silent.

Vance shrugged.

'You see? You had just enough sense to run away like this.' He slid the car into gear and started up the steep slope ahead of them. 'But what happens when you get back to Rome?'

'I'm not going back to Rome.' The words were out before she could check them, though she had had no intention of telling him of her decision.

Vance didn't seem to hear her. The car was slithering and jerking in the mud of the road which was little more than a track between fields.

'Damn! I can't hold her on this. Better see if I can turn in this gateway.'

For a moment their angry altercation ceased as he struggled to manoeuvre the car round until it was facing downhill again. He heaved on the brake and said, somewhat breathlessly,

'I was going to take you part of the way up to see the view, but it's too risky. We'd probably get stuck in this mud.'

She glanced towards the summit of the hill and saw the sky streaked with lemon and apricot colours where a watery sun was trying to break through. It glinted on the walls of the great Abbey, touching them to gold.

Vance leaned over and pushed at the door handle. He was so close she could feel his breath on her cheek, feel the warmth of his shoulder against hers, the black hair almost touching her chin.

'If you get out you'll be able to see better.' He slid his long legs on to the muddy verge and walking towards the open gateway, said over his shoulder, 'Come on.'

Something in the autocratic command triggered Jane off. A few moments ago she had been almost trembling with anger, so indignant was she at Vance's ill-considered remarks. Guileless and immature he had called her; an impressionable, gullible type. She stared at the back of his tall black head and a mad impulse came over her. She would show him. She would give him a good fright, shake him out of his lordly composure. Without stopping to think twice, Jane slid into the driving seat and released the brake. As the car moved slowly forward down the incline she turned on the ignition and the next moment the engine sprang into life and gathered up speed. She swung the wheel round, pressed her foot on the accelerator and set off down the hill at a fast speed.

She heard Vance shout—knew that he had turned and was running after her, but the car was moving more quickly with every second, and now, at a frightening speed, was careering towards the main road at the bottom.

The hill was steeper than she had realised. She tried to brake, to slow down, but the tyres were unable to grip on the mud and the wheels went slipping in the runnels of water streaming down the slope.

For the first time she had a sense of panic, an awareness that the car was now definitely running away with her. She wrenched at the steering wheel, trying desperately to turn the car into the undergrowth at the side of the road. Below her, coming nearer and nearer with every second, was the massive stone wall that ran along the bottom of the main road. A scream seemed to be rising in her throat. She pulled with all her strength at the wheel and as the car went bumping and racing over the stones and mud to the bottom of the hill, Jane, with one last tremendous effort, managed to turn the wheel a small amount so that the car reaching the level of the road swung round and ran waveringly for a few yards parallel with the wall. Then, with a thunderous crash that shook every bone in her body, it smashed into the stonework and came to a shuddering standstill.

CHAPTER FIVE

THE vibration, the tremendous jarring had stopped. She was floating, as if on the sea. Yes, there was the sail—that white moving thing, Jane thought muzzily, staring up with eyes that couldn't seem to focus properly.

The sail moved closer, bent towards her, and now it was wings. The wings of some bird. She closed her eyes, her head beginning to throb, and a gentle voice said, in Italian, '*Comè sta, signorina? Spero che stia meglia.*'

Jane opened her eyes again and saw that the bird was in reality a headdress, white and floating, and beneath it was a pale unlined face and deepset dark eyes. For a moment she didn't answer but just stared, and now she became aware that she was lying on a high narrow bed, and that she could not move her left arm which was encased in something hard and fixed at right angles to her body.

She tried to speak, but her mouth was stiff and bruised and the words came out with difficulty.

'*Mi sento male. Che cosa e successo?*'

A cool hand touched her forehead.

'You were in an accident, *signorina*. In the car that you were driving.'

Now she remembered. The terrifying rush down the steep track and being unable to stop the car; the struggle to turn the wheel and almost succeeding. But not enough. And the last crashing impact.

She shuddered and closed her eyes against the memory. Her head throbbed, every bone in her body seemed to ache. She tried to move her legs and found them confined in some sort of cage that held the bedclothes from them.

Jane had another remembrance and her eyes opened wide in alarm.

'Vance? Where is Vance?'

'Il fidanzato.' The white headdress nodded several times in assent. 'He is waiting to see you. I will bring him here.'

Jane put out her free hand, frowning against the word 'fidanzato', trying to make sense of it with a brain that felt as if it consisted of cotton wool. She said feebly,

'Fidanzato? I don't understand.' Her voice emerged a thread of sound and the Sister couldn't have heard her, for she moved out of sight and Jane was left alone.

But only for a few minutes. Someone came to the bedside and took hold of the hand that was lying limply on the cotton bedspread in a firm clasp and said,

'How are you, Jane?'

She blinked against the light and the light blotted out as the figure bent over the bed. Vance's deep voice said,

'Sister Teresa tells me you're on the mend. Thank goodness for that! You had me really worried for a while.'

He was so tall he dwarfed the small room; a black-browed stranger, yet, somehow, a strong reassuring presence.

'Wh-what happened to the car?' was all Jane could think of to say.

He sat down on the chair beside the bed and it gave a rickety protest as if about to collapse under his weight.

'I'm afraid it was a write-off. But don't worry about that. I shall fix something else up.'

She gulped, appalled by the enormity of her escapade.

'I'm so s-sorry. I didn't—I don't know why——'

He laid a finger against her lips.

'You're not supposed to talk. I'm just allowed in to say hello, and to let you know I'm around.'

She turned her head on the pillow and looked at him.

'Where am I?'

'In the private wing of a hospital at Cassino. Everything's being taken care of. You broke your arm, I'm afraid.' He reached forward and tapped the plaster. 'The reason for this contraption. And you cut your leg rather badly, but luckily, no break.' He smiled ruefully. 'And you knocked yourself out, of course. For about a week.'

Jane gave an involuntary gasp.

'I've been here a *week*? Oh, it's incredible. And you— you've had to stay here with me.' She said again, 'I'm so *sorry*,' and against her will the tears crept out and trickled down her cheek.

His finger came out again and gently smoothed the tears away.

'Now don't go to pieces on me or Sister will read the riot act and say I've been upsetting you. And don't worry about my hanging on here. I was all for killing time. Don't you remember? I'm arranging to hire a car and we'll go on in that. They tell me you'll be fit enough to move in another week.'

She laying staring up at the whitewashed ceiling, trying to think it all out. She had been here a week, and her arm was broken. But she would soon be able to leave. But where would she go to? She felt confused and muddled and terribly tired and the tears were threatening again. She made a great effort and said, as calmly as she could, 'Thank you for all you've done.'

He leaned towards her.

'You're not to worry about a thing. Promise. Just rest and get well. I've got an idea and I'll tell you about it when you're feeling stronger and able to talk.' He let go of her hand and stood up. 'Try and sleep now.'

She gave a sigh, half of relief, half of weariness.

'Yes.' Then she remembered something and said, lifting her head from the pillow. 'The Sister called you my—my *fidanzato*. Why—why did she do that?'

The wide shoulders shrugged.

'It made things simpler. The hospital, the police, they were fussing around so; passports, papers, names and addresses and details. I told them I was your fiancé, that we were to be married soon. It seemed easier that way. I had to go through your things—your luggage and so on. I apologise, and hope you don't mind!'

She turned her face away.

'How could I? The entire disaster was my fault.'

He patted the foot of the bed as he moved away.

'Not entirely. I provoked you—made you angry by the things I said. Admittedly your reaction was a bit drastic. But I'm to blame too. Now forget about it, and get well. 'Bye, Jane.'

The door closed behind him before she could summon her wits to answer. She closed her eyes and tried to think, but in a few moments she fell asleep.

Each time she slept and woke she felt better. She began to eat the simply prepared meals. The doctor came, a small bald-headed man who spoke no English, so it was lucky her Italian was fluent.

Vance came too, bringing a gift on each occasion; flowers, refreshing soap and toilet water, paperbacks and the attenuated British newspaper. Sister Teresa and her attendant nuns were overwhelmingly kind and they smiled and spoke admiringly of Jane's handsome, devoted '*fidanzato*'.

'He is good mans—strong, of much command,' said the youngest nun, whose English was somewhat limited.

'Yes,' Jane agreed. She was grateful to Vance and indeed had been surprised that someone she knew only slightly should act with such thoughtful generosity. But his kindness couldn't entirely obliterate the things he had said to her about Gino and his scornful remarks regarding herself. Her gratitude was mingled with a shadowy resentment which was no less strong for being hidden.

Now, sitting on the terrace in the warm autumn sunshine, a rug thrown over her knees, she thought of Gino again and wondered what his reaction had been to the letter she had left for him. Was he sad, as she was? Did he miss her as much as she missed him? The summer days, or rather evenings, they had spent together in Rome seemed like a dream now, a sweet and wonderful time she would never forget.

A shadow fell across the tiled floor and she glanced round to find Vance looking at her.

'Daydreaming?' His voice held its former sardonic note. 'You seemed to be miles away.'

'Was I?' She tried to sound casual.

He sat down on a nearby chair and leaned back, crossing his long legs.

'I'm afraid I must recall you back to earth to deal with more mundane matters. I've settled the hospital account for you. Sister says they're discharging you tomorrow.'

Jane stared.

'Tomorrow? I didn't realise.' She frowned. 'And—and the bill? D'you mean *you've*—paid it?'

He nodded, folding his arms across his broad chest.

'Naturally, as your *fidanzato*, it is my privilege. Now I want to talk to you about our plans.'

'But I must pay you back,' Jane insisted. 'The bill, I mean. How much was it? She hoped fervently that she would have enough in her bank account. From all she had heard the cost of private medical care in Italy was astronomical.

He shook his head.

'It's of no consequence. You see, I have this plan. In a way, a favour to ask of you. If you agree, we can call the debt quits.' He was frowning again. Something of his former abstracted manner had returned. He was less personal, less concerned for her.

'I'll do anything I can, of course,' Jane began.

One dark eyebrow lifted. 'Wait until you hear about it.' He paused, still frowning. 'You knew I was on my way to Corfu,' and at Jane's nod he added slowly, 'I'm going to stay with my brother. He has a house there. Also a'—there was another hesitation—'a wife and small daughter. He's been ill—a breakdown, from overwork, and has had to rest completely for several months. The thing is, we haven't seen each other for some time, not since my father's funeral two years ago, and in fact we've been estranged for longer than that.' He got up and walked to the edge of the balcony and stood staring at the mountains for a few minutes in silence. Then he turned and came back to stare down at Jane before continuing.

'I'm not explaining this very well. It's a complicated story, though the situation is commonplace enough. My father owned a large factory in the Midlands which manufactured component parts for machinery. It was extremely prosperous and he naturally wanted both his sons to go into it. Julian, my older brother, was quite happy to do so, although by temperament he's far from being a business type, but as my father ran the entire show, being a man of great drive and force, Julian fitted in very well on the sales side —a contact man to customers and business associates.'

Vance turned again and walked away, walked back, his face still darkened by a frown.

'When I left university I didn't want to go into the factory. I wanted to become a writer. My father was against the idea and he eventually talked me round. I felt I owed him something—he was my father, he had always been generous to both Julian and myself, so, very reluctantly, I started work in the factory. Father, of course, was one of those people who believed in working from the bottom up and so I went right through the grind of it all, something that Julian managed to escape because he was the "outside" man.

'Of course, it didn't work out. I honestly tried, but my heart wasn't in it. I longed for freedom and my father wanted to rule me in the way he always had done. There were faults on both sides—looking back, I can see that. I was selfish and headstrong, my father obstinate and dogmatic. My mother died when my brother and I were schoolboys and we were brought up by my father's unmarried sister who ran the house and gave in to him at every turn because she was so pleased to have such a comfortable home, plus a series of kindly foreign maids. Without the gentling influence of my mother, my father grew

65

harder and more set in his ways, he would brook no inter-
ference or opposition. In the end we quarrelled and I left
home and went my own way. As I said, it's a commonplace
enough situation.'

Jane looked up at him. 'And did you become a writer?'

'Yes. I was lucky. On the strength of some articles I'd
written, freelance stuff, I was given a job on a newspaper in
the north of England. After a bit I moved to Glasgow and I
finished up in London on a national newspaper. They sent
me to the States for two years and there I did a certain
amount of broadcasting, political reports and so on. Also
some T.V. work. After my father died I left the newspaper
and went to Australia and there I started to write a book.
It's to be published at the end of this year.' He met Jane's
absorbed gaze and said, almost impatiently, 'Oh, it's not
fiction—I doubt if it will become a best-seller or anything
like that. It's a bird's eye view of international politics, but
it's something I've wanted very much to write. However,
that has nothing to do with the present problem, which
concerns my brother.'

He paused.

'I said just now my brother was not a real businessman
by temperament. This didn't show up until after my father
died and he had to carry everything; make the decisions
and so on. The strain of this, the pressure of running the
factory proved too much for him and four months ago his
health cracked up, just at a time when the business was
planning to merge with an Italian firm with a view to Common Market expansion. A couple of weeks ago he wrote and
asked me if I would come to Corfu to see him and discuss
the business together. I still have some shares in it, left to
me by my mother. Julian wants me to go back into the firm
and help him out.'

'And will you?' Jane asked.

'I doubt it. I've been putting off the idea—marking time,
as I told you once—but I feel I must go and see him. I feel
guilty, in a way. Perhaps if I had stayed with the firm and

done my share Julian wouldn't have become ill.'

'And you didn't quarrel with *him*, did you? Only your father,' Jane said.

Vance made no answer and Jane, looking at him, saw the slate-grey eyes were hooded and expressionless as he stared past her as if to some shadow beyond.

At last he said slowly,

'There has been a rift between us, but over a—a personal matter. Not concerned entirely with the business.' His glance came back to her, and he gave her a direct look. 'Because of this—difficulty, it will be an awkward situation between us. I thought, if you came with me to Corfu, the whole thing would be less of a problem.'

Jane gazed at him in amzement.

'Go to *Corfu* with you—to stay with your brother and his wife, you mean? But surely that would be even more embarrassing? They don't know me—I'm a stranger—and from what you tell me the circumstances are already strained.'

'Believe me, damned strained,' Vance said curtly. He stared straight at her. 'I said I had a favour to ask of you, and here it is. And you said you wanted to settle a debt and this is the way you can do it. I know what I'm talking about. What do you say?'

Jane put a hand out.

'What can I say? I wrecked your car—you've paid my hospital bills—stayed here to look after me. I certainly owe you something. If you feel my going to stay with you at Corfu will help, then of course, I'll come.' She smiled slightly. 'It's no hardship. It's a place I've always wanted to visit.'

'I'm glad you feel that way, because there's one other stipulation.' His mouth twisted almost cynically, the grey eyes were cool and unsmiling on her own. 'I am still to be regarded as your *fidanzato*.'

She felt herself gape in astonishment.

'My fiancé? You're not serious!' and at his curt nod,

'But why—what on earth for?'

He hesitated.

'I have certain reasons which I don't want to go into. All I can say is, if you'll agree to act as if we were engaged to one another during our stay at my brother's villa, I shall be grateful and you'll have repaid any debt you feel you owe me.'

Jane was silent, biting her lip, as she considered the proposition. She was to pretend to be Vance Morley's fiancée while on a visit to his brother. What a fantastic idea!

'It will be a matter of a week or two at the most,' Vance went on. 'When we leave the island you'll be free of the engagement and able to go where you wish. It isn't as if you're expected anywhere else. You told me you hadn't been able to contact your friend in Naples and also that you didn't intend to return to Rome. You might just as well come to Corfu with me. Especially as with your arm in plaster you're not able to take on a job at present.' He looked at her. 'Of course, you could return to England—to your sister or friends. Had you thought of that?'

'I don't want to go back, not yet,' Jane said quickly. Somehow to return to England was to put too many miles between herself and Gino. Admittedly she was running away from him, but was that only for a respite? Did she hope in her heart that somehow, if she stayed in Italy, they would meet again, that somehow everything would come right?

The deep-cut mouth curled cryptically.

'I see Italy still holds an attraction for you. Well?'

'I've no real objection to—to your idea. Only—this pretence of being your fiancée seems so odd. We hardly know one another.'

'Then we shall have an excellent opportunity to improve our acquaintance.' There was a sardonic note in his voice which caused Jane to glance quickly at him. She opened her mouth to say, 'I don't think I can do it,' when he added, as if guessing her thoughts, 'The rented car is all fixed up ready to take us tomorrow. In place of my own.'

'Oh,' Jane said.

'You did rather wreck it, you know.'

She said sharply, 'That's blackmail. Making me feel guilty so I've got to agree to your idea.'

'What else?' He put a hand out. 'Shall we seal the bargain?'

She hesitated, then slowly put her hand into the firm well-shaped one outstretched towards her. Said slowly, reluctantly,

'All right, I'll go along with you.'

'Good. I'll make arrangements with Sister Teresa to collect you tomorrow morning.' He let go of her hand. 'Have a quiet day and rest all you can. 'Bye, Jane.'

Her thoughts were in a daze after he had gone. She was engaged to Vance and going to stay in Corfu with him. It was an incredible situation. She wondered what the reason for such makebelieve circumstances could be. It seemed extraordinary.

She shrugged to herself. Oh well, mystifying though it was, it was none of her business, and if enacting the role of a fiancée would repay all the money Vance must have spent on settling her account with the hospital, then she would gladly do it for the short time stipulated. Afterwards they would say goodbye to one another and most probably never meet again.

CHAPTER SIX

'WE'LL make Foggia for lunch,' Vance said as they turned off at Caserta on to the road signposted Benevento. 'There's a good hotel there, and we can rest for a bit. Then it's about a hundred and fifty miles to Brindisi where we catch the night ferry, to Corfu.' He looked round at her. 'Feeling all right?'

Jane nodded. Her arm was still in plaster, it would not come off for another two weeks. She felt curiously tired, although the journey had only just begun. Perhaps it was some sort of reaction to the accident. Even dressing this morning had been an effort, although Sister Maria, the little nun, had helped her and brushed Jane's long hair and tied it back with a ribbon so it wouldn't get in her way.

'Yes, thank you.'

'Just sit there and relax. Or close your eyes.'

She shook her head.

'I'm all right. I like seeing everything.'

He made no answer but looked back to the road ahead. It struck Jane that Vance too was oddly silent this morning and evidently had no wish for conversation. She stole a sideways glance at him as they drove along. He was frowning, black brows a straight bar above the narrowed grey eyes. His mouth was set grimly, the sensuous bottom lip pulled up against the top one to an almost sullen degree. He seemed lost in dark thoughts that excluded her presence. It seemed utterly incongruous that she was supposed to be his fiancée. She wondered with some trepidation what it would be like when they arrived at Corfu and hoped that Julian Morley would be less intimidating than his brother.

Luncheon at Foggia was a welcome break and Jane was glad to get out and stretch her legs, particularly as the injured one still felt stiff and painful after sitting. She went to the powder room of the hotel and tried to wash and tidy up with one hand. She hadn't realised it would be so awkward, for at the hospital one of the nuns had always been on hand to help her. She looked in the mirror at her pale face and shadowed eyes and was thankful that her hair had been fastened back for tidiness. She would have found it difficult to comb into smoothness if it had been left loose on her shoulders as was usual.

Vance was waiting in the foyer for her, and for a moment the look of introspection left his dark face and his expression softened slightly as he said,

'Let's have a drink before we eat.' He smiled so seldom that Jane was surprised how the flash of white teeth against his tanned skin and brightening of the cloud-grey eyes could change his looks. But when they sat down and he had ordered two Campari sodas he reverted to his former mood of preoccupation and conversation soon flagged.

The meal was excellent and revived Jane. Afterwards they sat for a long time over coffee as Vance insisted that she must rest in the big comfortable armchair before they resumed their journey.

'What time does the ferry leave Brindisi?' Jane asked as finally they returned to the car.

'About half past ten. We're in to Corfu at seven-thirty tomorrow morning.'

'I didn't realise it took so long.'

He nodded. 'Eight to nine hours. I've booked a cabin for you—you'll be able to rest.'

She looked at him.

'There was no need—I mean, I suppose people sit up. I could have done.'

He shook his head abruptly.

'Nonsense. You're hardly fit to travel as it is—you certainly couldn't do things the hard way. You really ought to have had another week in hospital.'

'Oh no,' Jane protested.

'Well, take things easy.' He held the car door open for

her and with some awkwardness because of the stiff leg she slid into the front seat. 'We've a long drive. Try and sleep some of the way.'

Jane protested that she couldn't, but whether it was the result of the luncheon or just sheer weariness, she felt herself beginning to nod off as Vance drove along and intermittently she slept.

At Bari they stopped again for a drink as they were both thirsty.

'Feeling better?' Vance said, as he offered Jane a cigarette and lit one for himself.

'Yes, much. I really slept—I didn't expect to.'

He stared at her for a moment, then he said abruptly,

'It's a pity we had that slight dissension earlier on. You've paid a high price for reacting with such vehemence to my well-meant advice. You could have been in Naples now with your friends instead of sitting here somewhat battle-scarred. I feel in part responsible.'

Jane's chin tilted defensively.

'There's no need. I feel responsible for wrecking your car. It was a pretty awful thing to do. But I thought we'd agreed the debts were settled?'

'Yes. It's just that——' He broke off and after a moment added, 'Does your—friend—what's his name, Gino? know you've run away from Rome?'

'I left a note for him.'

'Without a forwarding address, I trust.'

'What possible business can it be of yours?' Jane said sharply. She mastered her anger enough to say, 'You've asked me to pretend to be your fiancée while we're staying at your brother's villa. If we argue like this we won't even be on speaking terms by the time we get there.'

His smile was cryptic but not unkind.

'You could be right at that. Before we come to blows may I ask one more thing. Are you still in love with him?'

She hesitated, glancing away from his probing look.

'Two weeks isn't very long, is it? People don't—don't

change the way they feel as quickly as that.' She added in an almost inaudible voice, 'Even—even if they want to.'

There was a long silence. Then Vance said curtly, almost harshly,

'No. Sometimes people can't always change after a much longer period of time. As you say—even if they want to.'

Something in the tone of his voice brought her gaze back to him. He was frowning, staring past her in the moody introspective way she had come to recognise. In one sudden movement he jack-knifed to his feet, saying, 'Better get on. Another eighty miles to go.'

They walked back in silence to the car. Jane felt that Vance's abrupt change of manner and bitter way of speaking arose from personal experience. Perhaps he was in love with someone and things hadn't gone right for him? It was intriguing to speculate on what could have happened. Somehow he did not strike her as a man whose love affairs would go awry; he was so sure of himself, so certain. And, she had to admit, attractive in an oddly magnetic way. Surely whoever he fell in love with would love him in return?

The ribbon had slipped from her hair and the wind was blowing the long tresses, tangling them in a maddening sort of way. She tried with her one good hand to smooth them back and struggled to fasten the ribbon on again, but it was impossible. Vance, who had been at the boot of the car, checking something, came round and saw her.

'Here, let me help you.' He took the ribbon from her and caught hold of the brown mane of hair. 'Have you a comb?'

She fumbled in her shoulder bag and gave it to him and he began gently to comb her hair. As he lifted it off from her shoulders his fingers touched the nape of her neck. A curious shiver went through her at his cool but vibrant touch, it was like a small electric shock.

'Are you cold? I've a cardigan in the back of the car. Better put it on,' Vance said.

She shook her head. 'I'm all right.'

73

He finished combing her hair and tied it back with the ribbon.

Jane was wearing her suede jerkin over a dark blouse, the sleeve of which hung loose above the bulky plaster. Vance flicked a finger against the thin material.

'There's no warmth in it. I'll give you the woolly,' and he pulled open the car door for her. When she was in the front seat he took the cardigan and arranged it over her shoulders, saying, 'That's better, plenty of room to manoeuvre.'

'Thank you,' was all Jane could say. She settled back into the comforting warmth of the cardigan. It was fawn, cashmere, soft and somehow embracing. With the sleeves laid loose around her and the faint intangible scent of tobacco and shaving lotion rising from it she had a fleeting sensation of Vance holding her so. Then it was gone.

The mountains were left behind them now and the landscape under the fast darkening sky flattened as they ran along the coastline. It wasn't dark enough to see the country, but every now and then they passed through some small town and Jane would glimpse a garishly bright shop or café or the more dimly lit interior of a farmhouse.

'We can have dinner on board,' Vance said as at last they came to Brindisi and drove towards the ferry. 'Afterwards you'll be able to go to your cabin and rest.'

He had arranged to leave the hired car at the port to be collected next day, so when the various formalities had been completed they went aboard the small clean ship. Because it was October and almost the end of the season the vessel was not overcrowded. A smiling steward took them down a hatchway and along a narrow corridor to the cabin which Vance had booked.

'I'd better check everything's in order,' he said as they followed the man. 'Then I expect you'd like to freshen up before dinner.'

The steward held open the door and Jane walked into a minute two-berth cabin. Vance gave the man a tip and he smiled a thank-you and left them.

'Will you be comfortable here? Anything you need?' Vance asked, glancing round.

Jane couldn't speak. She was staring at the twin berths and Vance, seeing her startled glance, smiled sardonically,

'Don't worry. You're not expected to share this with me or anyone else. I got it for single occupancy by paying an extra half fare. So relax.'

Jane coloured, feeling faintly foolish.

'Have you a cabin too?' she asked as casually as she could.

He shook his head.

'Not worth it. There are plenty of seats comfortable enough to doss down on. And I like to prowl around a bit.' He turned to the door. 'I'll see you on deck, at the bar.'

'Yes. Thank you.'

There was nothing to unpack except night things and a toilet case. She was wearing suede pants which matched the jerkin, a convenient outfit in which to travel. She washed her hands and put on fresh lipstick and then made her way up to the main deck and the direction of the bar.

She saw Vance before he saw her. He was standing by the bar, staring moodily down at the glass in his hand. A lock of black hair fell across his frowning forehead; he looked remote and unapproachable. Jane hesitated in the doorway before bracing herself to go up to him. She reached his side and stood there several moments before he became aware of her presence. When he did so he stared blankly at her as if wondering who on earth she was, then he said jerkily,

'Sorry, Jane. I was miles away. What will you have to drink?'

He ordered a Cinzano for her and found seats where they could sit down.

'Everything O.K. below?'

She nodded. 'Yes. It's very comfortable, thank you.'

'Good.' He relapsed into silence again.

They finished their drinks and went into the restaurant where dinner was being served. When they had ordered Vance leaned back in his chair and said,

'I'm afraid I'm not very good company this evening.'

Jane looked across the table at him.

'Those problems? The ones you're running towards?'

His deep cut mouth twisted grimly.

'Yes. You're lucky—yours are behind you.'

Jane sighed. 'It doesn't mean they don't exist, because I've run away from them.'

'You mean you still hanker after the fellow?'

'I told you—people can't change to order.' She wanted to say, 'Is your problem a girl—are you in love with someone too?' but the glance of intimidating grey eyes checked her.

He said abruptly, 'Let's change the subject. If we have to talk about something, let's talk about your job. You haven't told me much about it, except that it's interesting and you enjoy it.' He shook his head. 'I can't imagine why. Carting coachloads of tourists around Rome, showing them the sights, telling them things half of them don't want to hear anyway. Didn't you get sick of it?'

'No, hardly ever. To begin with, I loved Rome and I enjoyed seeing all its wonders as much as the holidaymakers did. They only caught a fleeting glimpse of things, but I saw them over and over again and every time I saw some fresh aspect, something I hadn't seen before. And they weren't just tourists—they were people. I enjoyed their company—I was never lonely the whole season.' She stopped. 'Not—not until they all went home and the office closed. It was then for the first time I realised I was a foreigner.'

Because of Gino, she thought. Because I was outside his life, his *real* life, and I knew I didn't belong. That was when I felt lonely.

'I'm surprised you didn't find a boy-friend among the tourists, instead of falling for an Italian. There must have been plenty to choose from.'

'Not really. Unattached males, unless they're middle-

76

aged bachelors or elderly widowers, don't come on coach tours. And in any case it would never work. There's the time factor for one thing, and another is the other clients wouldn't like you seeming to be involved with one person—they'd feel it was taking the attention away from them that they should have.'

He looked at her.

'You carry quite a responsibility. What if something happens—an accident, someone falling ill, even dying?'

She smiled. 'We cope. We have to—it's part of the job. Complicated things can happen. For instance, in the early summer on one of the tour parties a girl fell ill—dangerously so. She had to go to hospital, and the awful part was, the man with her wasn't her husband and he just backed down and said it wasn't any of his business. In the end we had to send for her husband—there was nothing else to do.'

'What happened?'

'He took her back to England, but I don't know the rest.'

Vance shook his head. 'My God, what a situation!'

'Yes, frightful. But at least I haven't had someone die on me. That happened to Meg, the girl I shared the flat in Rome with. She's very experienced, fortunately. The woman was elderly and had a heart attack and died in the hotel where she was staying.'

'Was that in Rome?'

'No, Las Palmas. Meg was living in the hotel and she had to arrange everything, working with the Consul and the local authorities, of course. The husband and daughter were on the party and had gone out for the day, leaving the wife, who hadn't felt well, to rest in the hotel. Meg had to break the news to them when they got back—it was terribly sad.'

'What's the form when someone dies like that?'

'If it's a Catholic country like Italy, for instance, and the person who dies is a Catholic, they're usually buried there. Otherwise, the body is flown out.'

'You've successfully taken my mind off my own problems,' Vance said. His voice was dry.

'I didn't mean to sound depressing, but *you* asked the questions,' Jane answered.

'I know.' He smiled and once again she was struck by his change of expression. 'Don't worry. You've done me good, Jane.'

'I'm glad.' She smiled back at him. For a moment their glances locked and held and she was startled by the sense of intimacy between them—as if really they knew one another very well. Then Vance looked away and the impression was gone.

'We can have a walk round the deck before you go below,' Vance said as he signalled to the dining steward.

While they had been having dinner the ship had slipped its moorings and put to sea. The night was dark and windless. A thin beading of lights shone from the mainland, the air felt warm, almost sultry as if it still held the warmth of the African shore on its breath. They walked round the deck once or twice and then Vance took Jane below and said goodnight to her outside the cabin.

'We dock early. I suggest you have coffee and rolls brought to your cabin and then we can go straight ashore. I telephoned my brother from Cassino the night before we left and he'll send a car to meet us at Corfu.' He turned away, one hand raised. 'Sleep well.'

'Thank you. I hope you will too.'

She had forgotten how difficult it was to get undressed with one hand. The jerkin and blouse were manageable, but it was a struggle to get the suede pants off as they were close-fitting even with the zip unfastened. But she was undressed at last and washed and into a cool cotton nightdress. She left her hair tied back in the ribbon Vance had fastened and slid into the lower berth. For a little while she lay there thinking about Vance, wondering what problem was waiting for him at Corfu, and then the gentle motion of the ship as it made its way across the Adriatic sent her to sleep.

78

Jane woke to the ship's noise and bustle in what felt like the middle of the night. It was six o'clock. The cabin was an inside one, so there was no porthole to look out of. The smiling steward who had brought in her luggage last night appeared with coffee and rolls. He spoke very little English, so conversation was limited to a few phrases only.

Washing and dressing was again a problem. She packed the suede pants away, deciding that a skirt would be easier to get into. Then there was the difficulty of her bra. Last night she had managed to undo the hooks, but fastening them with one hand was a different matter. She struggled unsuccessfully and in the end was driven to pressing the bell to ask for a stewardess. Yesterday she had seen a white-aproned figure in the corridor, so knew there must be one in attendance somewhere.

After a long interval a tap came on the door and she called 'Come in.' The next moment she was clutching her silk kimono round herself, for the figure in the doorway was Vance.

Seeing her obvious discomfiture, he stared.

'Sorry. I thought you said "Come in." '

'I did. I—I thought it was the stewardess. I—rang the bell for her.'

'You're not dressed yet? Is there something you need? Can I help?'

Jane shook her head quickly.

'No, it's all right. Just—I——' She broke off as another tap sounded on the door. 'Yes?'

This time it was the steward. He looked questioningly at her, saying in his stilted English,

'Good mornings. You want somezings?'

'I rang for the stewardess.'

He shook his head. 'She—busy. Helpings old lady'—he gestured expressively—'put on clothes.'

Vance turned and said something in Italian and the man nodded and withdrew, closing the door behind him.

'Now,' Vance said, 'what's the trouble? If it's zipping up

you need I'm very handy at that sort of thing.' He eyed the blue silk kimono. 'Are you decent under that?'

'No—no, I'm not,' Jane said hurriedly. She bit her lip, wondering what to do, wondering how long the stewardess was likely to be. She swallowed. 'I—can't fasten something. If I—would you turn away for a moment, please?'

'Certainly.' Vance turned and stared with deliberation at the door. Jane quickly slipped of the kimono and pulled on a skirt over her pants, then slipped on the bra and held it to her. Then in a low voice she said, 'If—if you could just hook me up.'

She heard him turn, felt his fingers cool against her skin as he slid the shoulder strap over her injured arm and began to fasten the hooks of her bra. He said somewhat dryly,

'You wouldn't have this problem if you were Women's Lib. Anything else?'

'Just—just my blouse, please—it's on the chair.'

He laid it over her shoulders and over the plastered arm, then gently turned her round and began to fasten the buttons up the front.

'I don't know why you're so shy about all this,' he said. 'After all, if you were in a bikini on the beach I'd see a whole lot more of you.'

Still Jane couldn't meet his glance.

'I—I suppose so. It just seems—different.'

He shrugged.

'I can't think why. And as your fiancé, I'm sure I should be on fairly intimate terms with you.'

She coloured.

'But you—you're not really my fiancé. It's just a façade.'

'To us, yes. But to the rest of the world we must appear very much at ease with one another.' He paused and then added, 'Especially when we're at my brother's. So don't go too prim and Victorian on me, will you?'

Jane flashed a sudden upward glance at him, startled by his words. He was looking down at her, and he was no longer smiling. On the contrary, his expression was grim, the twist of his mouth cynical. She felt her heartbeat quicken, a sense of apprehension move in her, and for the first time she wondered what exactly she was letting herself in for.

CHAPTER SEVEN

JANE'S first thought as she saw the island was 'How green it is.' It looked so richly forested, so verdant. After the dryness of Italy, the aridity, Corfu was positively lush, with massive olive groves rolling like a silvery green river towards a sea so peacock a blue it dazzled the eye. And Corfu itself, cream and biscuit-coloured in the sun, with the great fortress dominating the town, the harbour gay with ships and yachts and ferries and small boats charmed her at first sight.

There were mountains too, their peaks amethyst against the sky and across the straits the bare hills of Albania shimmered in the morning haze. A small island lay beyond the harbour—the old quarantine island, Vance said briefly in answer to her question. He was seeing to the luggage, once more frowningly preoccupied, seemingly unaware of the sunlit beauty around him.

Jane was still staring at everything in bemused fascination when she heard a soft, almost caressing, voice speak Vance's name. She turned in time to see a girl in a pink trouser suit place a hand on each of Vane's arms and look smilingly up at him as she said,

'*Vance!* Vance, how wonderful to see you again! I can't believe it. How are you? You look well—so brown and strong. Hardly a day older.'

Jane did not hear Vance's reply—his voice was too deep and quiet. She tried not to stare, not to seem curious, yet before she glanced away she glimpsed the expression on his face—a look of startlement and something else. A frowning mixture of—anger, resentment, and—longing? Yes, that was the word. Yet, even as Jane looked quickly away, it had gone and his dark face was closed into polite impassivity.

The next moment she heard him call and turning her

head again, saw him coming towards her, one hand cupped under the arm of the girl beside him.

'Jane, I want you to meet Anthea, my—my brother's wife. She's very kindly come to meet us. And Anthea, this is——' He hesitated momentarily, then put his other hand out to Jane, catching hold of her fingers in his. 'This is Jane.' Again there was a pause, then he added slowly, 'We —we're engaged.'

For a moment the girl neither moved nor spoke. She stared blankly at Jane. Her eyes were a clear beautiful green under thin dark eyebrows, her hair dark and cloudy about the small oval face. She had red lips, a neat thin nose and a smooth creamy skin. She was lovely, and in the casual woven-cotton trouser suit, elegant.

She said uncertainly, '*Engaged?* But how wonderful! What fantastic news. But why didn't you say—why didn't you tell us—tell Julian when you spoke to him on the telephone? You simply said you were bringing someone with you; we thought you meant a man friend.' She laughed, a sharp high sound, then stopped abruptly, small white teeth catching the red underlip. 'I'm very happy for you both. That goes without saying. Welcome to Corfu, Jane.' She turned her head slowly in Vance's direction and said soberly, almost with an effort, 'Congratulations, Vance.'

He inclined his dark head, his fingers holding Jane's as if in vice. The pressure of his grip hurt, he seemed unaware that he was grasping her hand so tightly.

'Thank you.'

'But what have you done to your arm?' Anthea asked, her glance going back to Jane. 'Did you break it?'

Jane spoke for the first time.

'Yes. I—had an accident in Vance's car.'

'How shattering. I hope Vance wasn't driving.' She turned, not waiting for Jane's reply. 'The car's over here. Breakfast is waiting for you at the Villa. Shall we go?' and she led the way, walking quickly and gracefully along the Quay.

83

Vance let go of Jane's fingers; they were tingling painfully and she rubbed them unobtrusively as they walked behind Anthea to the parked car. It was a cream drophead coupé, sleek rather than roomy.

'Vance, you'd better sit in front, with your long legs. There's not much room at the back. Will you be all right there, Jane? It's only a short drive.'

In a few moments they were speeding out of Corfu, up a slight incline past the Royal palace and the famous Square where Jane had read that cricket was still played. The road swept round a wide tree-lined bay, there was a handsome park, statues, monuments, nursemaids sitting under the trees with their small charges scampering about their feet. A handsome hotel with Moorish-looking arches set among late roses and flowering shrubs was indicated by Anthea with a wave of her hand as the Corfu Palace, then they drove past more gardens and some charming old houses, Anthea turned right and they were in a poorer, less elegant district.

Soon they had left the town and the airport behind them and were among the olive groves which lined the mountainsides. There were cypress trees too, tall and sentinel, so dark a green as to look almost black against the cloudless sky. Now the sea came into view again, a deep kingfisher blue, and lying upon its dazzling surface, the small bright jewel of Pontikonisi.

Vance turned his head.

'Are you all right there, Jane?'

She nodded, scarcely taking her enthralled gaze from the beauty opening up before her.

'Yes, thank you. It—it's fabulous!'

He looked back to the road. Anthea was driving with speed but precision along the curving winding road, its surface rutted and potholed from the rigours of new building. Jane could see signs everywhere; hotels set into the steep mountainsides, with curving ascents up to them; new villas in pockets of land scooped out of the forest, a cottage perched high above the road commanding a spectacular view.

Yet, somehow, it remained miraculously unspoiled, the sheltering olive trees softening intrusion, hiding scars.

They came to a high stone wall with tall trees reaching above it, hiding the view of the sea, and Anthea slowed the car to turn in between double wrought-iron gates. The drive curved, sloping down to a blue-tiled roof and in another minute they reached a low cream-washed house surrounded by a paved patio. Urns and tubs planted with geraniums and petunias flaunted bold colour; the purple bougainvillea was still in bloom and late roses grew in profusion against the walls of the house. Part of the building looked old, the stonework mellowed and crumbling, but one wing seemed to have been added recently. Nevertheless, the blending was harmonious and the whole place had a homely welcoming look, with steps going up and down to different levels, hiding an aspect here, revealing a vista there.

Anthea gestured towards an open doorway, at the side of which hung a ship's bell on a wrought-iron bracket.

'Please go in. Julian will be waiting for you.'

Jane went through, followed by Vance. They were no sooner in the cool tiled hall furnished with an immense carved chest on which stood a bowl of headily scented stocks than a figure appeared in an archway at the far end. A tall man, his face in shadow, stood staring at them for a moment before coming slowly towards them, one hand outstretched.

'Hello, Vance. It's good of you to come.'

Vance said stiffly, 'How are you, Julian?' He shook hands. 'I hope you're feeling stronger.'

'Thanks—I'm better than I was.'

Julian was like Vance but thinner and slighter in build, and his eyes, which were blue instead of grey, held an expression of nervous uncertainty.

As his glance moved to Jane, Vance slid an arm about her shoulder and said, 'This is Jane. We're going to be married.'

Julian's surprise was as great as Anthea's had been, except that the first look of startlement was replaced by one of genuine pleasure.

'*Married?* You mean—she's your *fiancée?*' He lifted a thin hand to brush back a lock of light brown hair. 'Good heavens, Vance, why didn't you say something about this before? You're going to be married? I can't credit it.' He took Jane's uninjured hand in his and bent to kiss her cheek. 'Lovely to meet you, Jane.'

'Th-thank you,' was all Jane could say, and that with the stiffness of unreality. She couldn't believe this was all happening—meeting Vance's family as his fiancée. She was very conscious of his arm about her, the pressure of his fingers on her shoulder, as if in warning.

Julian turned to Anthea, who had remained standing by the wooden chest, ostensibly looking at some paper or letter left there.

'Darling, isn't this the most incredible piece of news? We thought Vance was a confirmed bachelor by now, didn't we?'

Anthea came slowly towards them.

'Did we? We're certainly surprised.' Her eyes, oddly watchful, held Jane's glance. 'Have you and Vance known each other long?'

While she hesitated, Vance answered for her.

'Oh, not very long. It was love at first sight.' He bent his head towards Jane and brushed a kiss on her hair. His fingers tightened menacingly into her shoulder. 'What you might call a whirlwind romance, wasn't it, sweet?'

Jane swallowed, startled by the touch of his lips.

'Y-yes, I suppose it was.'

'How romantic,' Anthea drawled. 'But of course, Vance, you always were a romantic person.'

Julian glanced round at her, and then at Vance. He said uncertainly,

'Shall we go in to breakfast?' He gestured for Jane to

walk ahead, and she went under the archway and down a flight of shallow steps into a wide and beautiful room. It was furnished in modern style with low archairs and curving settees. Colourful Turkish rugs lay across the polished floor. The walls were off-white and an enormous chimney breast of stone with a fireplace laid with logs filled one wall, half hiding a gallery which ran round the room. This was reached by a spiral staircase of wrought iron built at one end, where a circular table, standing near one of the windows of sliding glass, was laid for the meal, indicating the dining area.

'Do sit down,' Anthea said. 'I've told Hestia to bring in the coffee.'

Jane sat down, still feeling slightly dazed, but already charmed by her new surroundings. The windows looked out on to another terrace which was built out over the sea and commanded a view of dazzling blue water and tawny-hued mountains. A caique with red and white sails moved slowly on the water, while inshore, a power boat came ptt-ptting into view, a tautly poised figure skimming the ripples of waves in its wake.

A neat young girl in a dark dress brought in coffee, there was melon or grapefruit to eat, followed by lightly scrambled eggs. The scent of roses and stocks drifted in through the open window. To Jane it was all like a dream.

Julian's voice brought her back to reality.

'When are you two going to be married?' he asked.

'We've not settled an actual date yet,' Vance said. 'It depends on several things—for instance, how long I'm likely to stay on Corfu.'

Julian looked at him frowningly, his blue eyes puzzled.

'You could be married from here, if you wanted to. We'd like that, wouldn't we, Anthea?'

Anthea, appealed to again, seemed to tense, sitting silent for a moment. Then she shrugged.

'You must leave Vance to make his own arrangements. It's enough that he's come here to help with your business problems.' She looked at him, her voice and expression softening. 'I don't need to tell you how grateful we are. Julian's been at the end of his tether—quite unable to cope.' She put a pale slim hand on his arm. 'Thank you for coming.'

He stared down at the long fingers, saying stiffly,

'I'll be glad to help if I can. But don't count too much on me. I've been out of the business for some time now.'

'Perhaps, but you knew it backwards. You went through the whole thing, I remember. Julian didn't do that—he was only on the sales side.'

'The most important—getting the orders. No use running a factory unless you have those coming in all the time.'

'That's true,' Julian broke in. He leaned forward, his anxious face brightening. 'That's what I tell Anthea. My job was to get new business—I was never trained to run the technical side. I admit that after Father died I couldn't cope with the management aspect, but that wasn't my fault. Father had always run the factory *his* way—no one else had any say in things.'

'No one's blaming you,' Anthea said coolly. 'You did your best, but it needs someone like Vance to cope with this Italian merger.' She broke off. 'Anyway, time enough for you two to discuss the whole affair. I'm sure it must be most boring for Jane.'

Vance reached out to pat Jane's hand.

'Jane knows all about the situation, naturally enough, as my wife-to-be.' His grey eyes seemed to mock Jane for a moment as he met her glance. 'She's a competent girl herself. Held down quite a responsible job in Rome, didn't you, Jane?'

Jane coloured slightly.

'I had certain duties, yes.'

'What *was* your job?' Anthea asked. 'And where was it?'

'I was a—a courier with a tourist agency. In Rome.'

For a moment Anthea looked blank, then she laughed.

'No? Not *really*. You mean one of these—what do they

88

call them—package deal things? How amusing. What did you have to do?'

'All manner of things,' Jane said calmly. 'And I enjoyed every minute of it.'

Anthea shrugged slim shoulders.

'Why not? It sounds a fun thing.' She smiled round at Vance. 'Don't tell me *you* were one of Jane's customers—clients—whatever they call themselves. That I *can't* believe.'

'No, I wasn't on a tour. But we did meet in Rome. As I said before, it's been a very romantic courtship.'

Anthea was staring at him, a frown puckering her smooth forehead.

'You met in Rome? But that must have been terribly recently. When you answered Julian's letter you wrote from an Australian address—Perth, wasn't it?'

'Yes. I was living there—I'd been writing a book.'

She brushed aside the reference to his writing.

'But it was September when Julian wrote. Had you met Jane before then—I mean *before* you went to Perth?'

Vance shook his head.

'No. We met in Rome. As you said just now, quite recently. I forget exactly when. Late September, perhaps, or October. Do you remember, Jane?'

'N-not the exact date.'

Anthea's cool green eyes narrowed.

'I always knew you were impulsive, Vance, but this time you've surpassed yourself.'

'It happens every day. People falling in love at first sight.' Vance's voice hardened. He stared directly back at Anthea. 'But then you wouldn't know about that, would you? You and Julian knew one another so well before ever you decided to get married.'

For a moment she met his glance and then she looked away, her creamy skin seeming to grow a shade paler. Julian's hand lying on the tablecloth opened and closed in a jerky movement, his mouth set thinly. The tension was almost audible, like a ticking clock cutting into the silence. Then, with one swift movement, Anthea stood up.

'If we've all finished breakfast perhaps Jane would like to see her bedroom. Nestor will have carried the cases in from the car. Shall we go, Jane?'

Jane jumped up with a feeling of relief. She didn't know what all the undercurrents of conversation implied, but of one thing she was sure; much more lay under the surface of these people's lives than might ever be revealed. This was why Vance had instigated the masquerade between Jane and himself. As a cover-up. For what?

The bedroom Anthea showed her to was a small charming room overlooking another aspect of the garden. It was simply but attractively furnished with a pretty cane-headed bed and frilled white bedspread and rose and white rugs on a polished floor.

'I hope you've everything you need,' Anthea said. 'There's a bathroom next door shared with the other guest room.' She frowned, staring round abstractedly as if thinking of other matters. Then she said abruptly, 'Come to the terrace when you're ready.'

'Thank you,' Jane said.

When Anthea had gone Jane stepped out on to the balcony and saw the garden below; a patch of lawn with a sprinkler pearling water across its green. A massive fig tree grew in one corner, dahlias, zinnias and marigolds splashed colour in another, a low yew hedge formed a boundary.

For a few moments she stood there, looking but only half seeing. How strange it was that she should have come here with a man she scarcely knew and on such seemingly intimate terms. She put a hand up to her shoulder, as if she could still feel Vance's hard grip. He had kissed her hair. She had been so startled at the time that she would have jumped backwards if he had not held her so firmly to him.

She pushed the thought of him away and went back into the bedroom and began to unpack her suitcase, hanging up the few dresses she had brought, along with a cotton jersey pants suit and a skirt and some sweaters. It wasn't a very imposing array; remembering Anthea's elegance and the quiet expensiveness of the Villa Tyche, Jane felt inadequately provided for. Oh well, she didn't suppose she would be staying here for long.

It was time to go down. Hesitantly she made her way back to the living-room, only to find it empty. She went out on to the terrace, into the glittering morning. The view was breathtaking, the jewel-bright sea, a myriad blues. Deep turquoise here, dark indigo there, sparkling sapphire on the horizon while inshore it changed to pale amber over the stones and was so crystal clear Jane could see seaweed, pinkish and feathery moving in the gentle wash of the waves.

She walked along the terrace which curved with the promontory upon which the villa was built. A stone parapet guarded against the drop below. Oleanders and hibiscus grew against the wall of the house, while under a golden-leafed tree green-cushioned chairs and green-cushioned loungers were set out, with a matching green umbrella above low tables.

A voice from behind said 'What's your name?' and swinging round Jane saw a small girl of about four in a pink checked dress staring at her.

She smiled. 'I'm called Jane. What is yours?'

The child came slowly towards Jane, staring up at her out of blue eyes, very like Julian's.

'Judy. It's short for Ju–diff.'

'What a pretty name.' She had Anthea's dark hair, it curled about her small head in a charming fashion.

'I live here,' Judy announced.

'Aren't you lucky? It's a wonderful place to live. Do you paddle in the sea?'

'I *swim*.' Judy's voice was scornful. She went to the edge of the terrace and pointed. 'In the pool—it's down there.'

Jane went to stand beside her and looking over the edge of the stonework she glimpsed another terrace below them

91

and the curving outline of a swimming pool with a paved surround and blue and white chairs and a gay little blue and white changing pavilion. Leaning further over, she made out some steps leading down to a rocky beach and a boat-house and a jetty.

She looked to the right and saw the mountains, green with olive groves and pine trees and cypress, coming down to meet the shining blue sea, saw coves and headlands and a gleam of pink and yellow houses rimming a small bay.

She turned back to Judy with a sigh.

'I've never seen anything so beautiful.'

Julian's voice answered her.

'That's what everyone says. But it's true. Elizabeth of Austria who built the Achilleon called it the most beautiful spot on earth, and she was an inveterate traveller, as you probably know.' He smiled, the look of nervous anxiety lifting momentarily. 'I see you and Judy have become acquainted.' He put a thin hand out and ruffled the dark curls. 'Where's Mummy, poppet?'

Judy took hold of his hand and with her other gestured vaguely.

'She went down there—with the man.'

'To the pool?' Julian glanced at Jane. The *man* obviously was Vance. 'Would you like to go down?'

'Yes, it would be nice.'

Judy gave a tug and started to lead her father along to where two urns filled with pelargoniums showed a break in the balustrade and steps led down between summer jasmine and blue and mauve Morning Glories. Julian paused at the top to wait for Jane, and they walked down side by side, Judy hopping and skipping two steps at a time ahead of them.

There was no one in sight by the pool. Julian shrugged.

'I expect Anthea's taken Vance to the beach. Shall we sit down and wait for them? It's rather a steep climb back— I'm apt to fight shy of it.'

Jane sat down on one of the striped chairs, leaning back

with a sigh of pleasure.

'It's so warm—like midsummer. Is it always like this?'

'It usually is in October—the rains come next month, though even then we get some beautiful days.' He smiled wryly. 'This green isn't here for nothing—it's the greenest island in the Mediterranean.'

'Have you lived here long?'

'We've had the Villa for four years—it was an old place, quite simple. We've added to it—built on, and modernised, I think without spoiling it.' He shook his head. 'We only used it for holidays—never during the winter. But this year' —he shrugged again—'I don't know. We may stay until spring, until I'm absolutely fit again.' He frowned. 'Of course, it's rotten for Anthea—very dull for her. Luckily she has a friend living in Athens whose husband is attached to the American Embassy there and she goes over to stay with them from time to time. She and Kay are old friends, they were at school together. Kay has two children, a daughter of eight and a boy about Judy's age, so that's a great asset. They come and stay with us here.'

'Judy's a darling—and so pretty,' Jane said.

The thin face softened.

'Yes. She's the dead image of Anthea, as you can see. You like children, Jane?'

'Very much.'

'So do I. I'd like a son—I hope—well, of course, at the moment Anthea's got her hands full looking after me. But later——' His voice trailed off, then he said more briskly, 'I can't imagine Vance with kids. He's so undomesticated ... always been footloose and fancy free.' He leaned forward and said with sudden seriousness, 'I'm glad he's found you, Jane. Very glad you're going to marry him. It will be a good thing in—in every way.'

Jane went tense and straightened up. She looked away from Julian's intent gaze.

'Th-that's very nice of you,' was all she could find to say.

93

'I mean it. You're just the girl for him. Pretty, sensible—adaptable I should imagine. Well, you'd have to be, holding the sort of job you've had. Yet you're ready to settle down and have children—you say you love them.' He nodded. 'You're the best thing that could happen to Vance.'

Jane was too uncomfortable to reply. She felt an utter fraud. Here was Julian saying all these nice things about her, and nothing that he thought about her and Vance was true. Thankfully she heard the sound of voices and jumped up, saying hurriedly,

'I think I hear someone coming. Yes, here they are,' and waved as Vance and Anthea appeared at the top of the steps leading from the beach, with Judy running ahead of them.

She said breathlessly, 'I fetched them, Daddy.'

'Good.'

'Hello,' Anthea said. Her voice was abrupt, her expression oddly set. 'Have you two been amusing one another?'

Julian held out a hand towards her.

'Yes, we've been getting better acquainted. Come and sit down, darling. You look hot.'

Anthea ignored his gesture.

'I'm going to wash my hands. The boat's dirty.'

Vance moved towards Jane and slid an arm round her waist.

'How's my girl?' he enquired affectionately. 'Missed me?'

For a moment Jane was too stunned to speak. She stood within the circle of Vance's arm, aware of his hold on her, aware of his cool grey gaze. Aware of Julian's approving smile up at them, of Judy hopping up and down on the paving nearby. Aware most of all of Anthea's glance at her, narrowed, and there was no other word for it, resentful. Julian might approve of her as Vance's future wife, but it was more than obvious that Anthea did not.

94

CHAPTER EIGHT

DURING the next few days Jane saw little of Vance. He shut himself up in Julian's study, sometimes with Julian, but mostly, as Julian was not fit to endure such intensive sessions, on his own. At meal times he was frowning and preoccupied, and in the afternoons when Julian took a siesta, Vance disappeared down to the beach to swim or sunbathe. He made a show, obviously for appearances' sake, of wanting Jane to accompany him, but when they were alone together on the beach he paid little attention to her. If he was not swimming much further out than Jane dared attempt with her injured arm, he would lie supine with his eyes closed as if asleep or sit under an umbrella, his muscular body above the bathing trunks already browned to teak colour by the Australian sun, poring over a sheaf of papers, oblivious of her presence.

Once he glanced up and saw her lying on the rocky ledge nearby and frowned, saying, 'Hello. You still there?' He took off the black glasses he was wearing and stared at her, his eyes lightened to pewter colour against the tanned skin. 'I'm sorry, I'm afraid I'm poor company.'

'That's all right. You've work to do. I understand.'

'I'm afraid it's dull for you. Why don't you and Anthea go off for the day, sightseeing somewhere?'

Jane shook her head quickly, uncomfortably aware that Anthea was not friendly towards her. It was hard to pin down the sensation to any actual cause, she just knew they were not on the same wavelength. The idea of a day out together made her feel nervous.

'I'm quite content here. It's gorgeous to laze in all this sun. And I walk quite a bit—sometimes with Judy and the donkey. We go through the olive groves. I find it wonderful that nowhere is enclosed, that you can wander at will.'

'Yes. The island's amazingly unspoilt. I don't know how long such a state of things will continue.' He slid his glasses on again. 'Well, as long as you're happy,' he said, and looked down again to the papers on his knee.

Happy? Jane thought, staring up at the cloudless sky. Not exactly that. She was still too hung up over Gino to be happy; she thought too much and too often of him. The summer in Rome seemed like a magic interlude. Would she ever see Gino again? Did he think of her too sometimes and wonder where she was and how she was?

He would imagine she had returned to England. If he heard from Enrico Baldoni that she had not accepted the job that Signor Baldoni had offered her and he didn't see her again at any of the places which had been so familiar to them both he would conclude that she had left Rome.

Here on this island, so strangely peaceful with its almost fairytale ambience, Jane felt suspended in time. As if she was stationary between two sets of happenings—those she had experienced and the ones still to come. It was a curious almost unreal feeling.

A few mornings later Vance came in search of her.

'I'm leaving for Milan in the morning. I can't settle everything by phone, so I'm flying to Athens and thence to Italy. You'll be all right here with Anthea and Julian, won't you?'

She had an odd feeling of dismay. She might not be in close contact with Vance, but he was familiar, he was *there*.

'Yes, I—of course. Will you be gone long?'

'A few days. The manager of the factory is flying out from England to help clear up some problems.'

'Yes, I—I see.'

He frowned down at her. 'What about that arm of yours? Isn't it about time the plaster came off?'

'I suppose it is. It's beginning to feel frightfully itchy.'

'I'll take you to Julian's doctor this evening. Before dinner.'

She was aware of a faint resentment caused by the

96

abruptness of his voice, but quelled the sensation, realising that Vance only meant to be helpful. All the same, she had the feeling of being just another item on the agenda to be dealt with and then crossed off.

'Thank you. I'll be ready.'

Dr. Karalis lived in a tall Venetian style mansion behind the Royal Park of Mon Repos. He was a charming elderly man with beetling black eyebrows above piercing black eyes and a shock of iron-grey hair. In no time at all he had cut the plaster from Jane's arm and pronounced the break excellently healed. He prescribed a few simple exercises for her to do to help restore mobility to the joint and suggested that she return to see him in a couple of weeks' time.

'What bliss to be free of that encumbrance!' Jane declared with a sigh of relief as she and Vance walked down the steps to where Vance had driven her to Corfu in Julian's car, for at the last moment it had been arranged that Julian and Anthea would come in later to Corfu to meet Vance and Jane for dinner at the Corfu Palace Hotel.

This had been Anthea's idea. When she heard that Vance was taking Jane to see Dr. Karalis, she had immediately suggested dinner in Corfu.

'We must *do* something,' she had declared gaily. 'It's been all work and no play for everyone and poor Jane will be bereft when you go off tomorrow.' Her voice was sympathetic, but her green eyes were fixed on Vance's face. 'We shall all miss you, you know that, Vance.'

Vance made no answer. His manner with Anthea was aloof, often abrupt to the point of rudeness, and there were times when Jane wondered if in fact Vance did not care greatly for his sister-in-law. Yet Anthea never seemed to mind; she was always gentle and charming, her voice would drop to an almost pleading note as if she was determined not to be offended. It was curious, for with Julian and Jane, and even to small Judy, she could be casual and offhand.

It was dusk as they drove towards the hotel. The sun had gone down in a pearly sky, pink behind the mountains, and the lights were shining along the curve of the Bay.

Julian and Anthea were already there, waiting in the bar with a drink on the table before them. Anthea looked particularly beautiful this evening in a trouser suit of emerald green Thai silk. Jane, in a simple tricel dress, felt somewhat inadequate for such sumptuous surroundings; everyone else seemed expensively or elegantly dressed, although not always at one and the same time.

'How's the arm?' Julian enquired as he sat down beside Jane.

'As good as new, so they tell me.'

'That's nice to hear.'

'Yes.' Unexpectedly the remembrance of Vance coming to the cabin that morning and hooking her up came into Jane's mind and he glanced across and his eyes met hers. He smiled, almost mockingly.

'It had its problems, didn't it, Jane?'

She felt herself colour. 'Yes.'

Julian glanced at her and then at Vance.

'Such as?' he enquired.

'Oh, getting dressed. Jane had trouble with hooks and eyes, didn't you, Jane? And hair—I seem to remember combing your hair for you.'

Anthea's green eyes narrowed as she looked at Jane.

'That's the snag of long hair—it gets untidy so quickly.'

Vance, who was sitting the other side of Jane, put a hand out and wound a tress of her brown hair up on to his fingers.

'Oh, I don't know. It's very pretty.'

His hand touching the back of Jane's neck seemed, for no accountable reason, to burn into her skin. Yet curiously she felt an imperceptible shiver go through her as if she was cold.

Anthea's expression, without appearing to change, hardened, and once again Jane was aware of a hidden tension, an antagonism between her and Vance. She was right. It must be that they disliked one another but masked it for

Julian's sake.

They ate dinner in the handsome restaurant overlooking Garitsa Bay, dark now except for the lights from a passing ship or fishing boat. An orchestra was playing, there would be dancing for those who wished, but Jane, remembering the gay wonderful evenings with Gino in the Trastevere, thought how set and decorous this all seemed.

Perhaps Vance thought so too, for he was frowning and restless, the moment of lightness when he had championed Jane gone. After coffee they walked through the gardens of the hotel to the beautiful swimming pool in its walled and semi-tropical setting. There were lanterns in the trees and the wind off the sea was pleasantly warm.

Jane found herself beside Julian. He was quiet and she knew he was tired, for towards the end of dinner his thin face had looked drained. Most evenings at the Villa Tyche he went to bed early, and she guessed that working so much with Vance this past week had exhausted him.

He said now, 'You'll miss Vance when he's away.'

She brought herself back into the act.

'Yes, very much. I might explore some of the island to help fill in the time.'

'Anthea'll show you around.' He gave a sigh. 'I'm sorry I'm not up to doing much.'

'I don't want to be a nuisance,' Jane said hurriedly. 'I might rent a little car.'

'You can borrow the Sunbeam—or Anthea's. I take it you've an international driving licence?'

'Yes—but I shouldn't like the responsibility of using one of yours.' She added, 'Especially after what happened last time.'

'You mean when you drove Vance's? That must have been a bad smash—he said the car was a write-off.'

'Yes.' Jane bit her lip at the remembrance. 'Perhaps I'd better borrow a bicycle,' she finished lightly.

Julian turned his head. In the half darkness he looked more like Vance—the same height and well-shaped head,

99

but his shoulders were narrower, his build slighter.

'I wonder where the other two have got to?'

'I think they're still by the pool. Yes, I can see them.'

Julian was frowning. 'We ought to be getting back to the Villa—Vance won't want to be too late if he has to catch the early plane to Athens.'

'Shall I tell them?' Wanting to help Julian who had sat down on one of the wrought iron seats, Jane went towards the pool. The two figures were still standing on the tiled surround, staring down at the water as into a mirror. As Jane came across the grass she saw Anthea turn and put a hand on Vance's arm and heard her say in a low unexpectedly sweet voice,

'Have you forgotten, then? I haven't. I never shall.'

Jane halted abruptly, aware that she had come upon two people in a close, almost intimate conversation. Then, not wishing to seem an eavesdropper, she called out,

'Vance, are you there? Julian thinks we should be leaving soon.'

Anthea's arm dropped from Vance's arm—they turned together and Vance moved a step forward.

'Sorry, were you looking for us?'

Jane came up to the pool, saying as casually as she could,

'No one having a moonlight bathe? It looks most inviting.' Without glancing at either Vance or Anthea she added, 'Julian seems very tired.'

'Yes, of course,' Vance said. 'We'd better go. I've some last-minute things to see to when I get back, as it happens.'

Jane walked after his tall figure, aware that Anthea hadn't moved, but was still standing by the pool. Her words seemed to echo in Jane's mind, the almost caressing note of her voice as she had said 'Have you forgotten, then? I haven't. I never shall.'

Puzzling. Puzzling and curious. Whatever antagonism lay between Anthea and Vance it was not on Anthea's side. She sounded entirely friendly. More than friendly. Affectionate? Then it must be Vance who was at odds with *her*.

100

They drove back to the Villa separately, Anthea taking Julian, Vance with Jane. Vance was silent the entire journey back to the Villa Tyche, and Jane, after one sideways glance at his aloof dark face, could not bring herself to start any conversation.

Julian, tired and yawning, went off to bed at once. Anthea lingered for a while moving restlessly about the room, sipping at a drink she had poured for herself, glancing frequently in the direction of Vance, who lounged in an armchair, frowning over his glass.

At last he rose abruptly, saying, 'I've some things to see to. Goodnight, Anthea. Look after Jane for me. I shall have left in the morning before anyone is up except Hestia.' He put a hand out towards Jane. 'Coming?'

She put her hand uncertainly into his outstretched one and allowed herself to be led from the room, calling over her shoulder,

'Goodnight, Anthea. It's been a lovely evening.'

Outside the study he released his hold on her fingers to open the door. When Jane hesitated, he gave her a push and she went in, turning nervously as he closed the door behind him.

'Did—did you want to speak to me?'

His mouth curled cynically,

'My dear girl, this is the moment for a lovers' farewell. I'm leaving you for nearly a week.'

She stared at him, found herself backing into the desk and at the sight of her dismay he gave a short laugh.

'Heavens, I'm not serious! I brought you in here for the look of the thing. Don't you suppose as I'm your devoted fiancé Anthea expects me to kiss you a passionate goodnight and goodbye somewhere? We'll have to hang around here for a few minutes.' He held out a silver case. 'Cigarette?'

His coolness unnerved her. For a moment she had been apprehensive, wondering what was about to happen, and then this curt businesslike approach. To cover her confusion

101

she turned away and sat down on the arm of a chair and said as calmly as she could,

'I—I suppose so.'

He crossed to the desk and picking up a sheaf of papers, glanced through them with frowning absorption. A small gilt carriage clock on a bookshelf ticked through the ensuing silence, and as the minutes went by Jane felt a mounting exasperation. Really, he was unconcerned to the point of rudeness. She might just as well not be here at all. Except from the point of view of his plan to have her regarded as his fiancée. And really, what on earth *for*? Vance had said that by bringing her here an awkward situation would be avoided, but Jane couldn't see it. Apart from a stiffness of manner and a certain reserve, the relations between the two brothers seemed normal enough. The entire masquerade appeared to be pointless.

Vance looked across to the clock, put the papers down on the desk and said curtly,

'That should do the trick.'

Jane felt herself beginning to explode.

'What is the *reason* for all this? I don't understand. It seems stupid and unnecessary.'

The black brows came down over the narrowed grey eyes. Vance said coldly,

'The reasons don't concern you. Just play the part allotted to you. That was the bargain.'

'But it seems absurd——' Jane began, and then broke off, aware of a formidable anger in the frowning face above her. She stood up, bracing herself against some onslaught. But he moved away from her and went towards the door, saying in the same cold voice,

'I don't wish to discuss it. All I ask is that you keep your word over our arrangement. In another week or two you'll be able to leave here—we shall leave together—and then you'll be free to think and do as you please. Goodnight.' He pulled open the door and stood aside to let her pass through.

She glanced quickly up at him, as if in apology, but the steel-grey eyes stared over her head. All she could do was stammer,

'Yes, all right. I—I shall do my best to—to act as we agreed. Goodnight, Vance.'

The door closed behind her and she stood for a moment in the tiled hall, wondering where Anthea was, if she was within earshot. There was no sign—the living-room was empty, unlit. Slowly Jane went up the stairs to her bedroom, thinking of Vance and the dark anger in his face when she had questioned him. He had looked at her as if she was a stranger, an intruder; as if she was trying to discover something he wished to keep hidden.

There was something, of course. She realised that now. But what it was she was sure she would never know. At least, Vance was not likely to tell her. Soon, as he had said, she would go away from the Villa Tyche and they would never meet again.

Strange interlude, Jane thought. A stopping-off point between the parting from Gino and—what? Where would she go from here?

She made a small movement of her head as if shaking away the sense of sadness, of uncertainty that threatened her, and went along the silent landing to her bedroom.

At last Jane was able to swim properly. It was wonderful to go out well beyond the shallow waters of the beach and swim and float in the deep waters further out. Wonderful to gaze back at the olive groves, running like a grey-green sea to meet this other sea, to see the curving coastline, the dot that was Mouse Island, to pick out the Villa Tyche, a cream speck among the trees, its blue-tiled roof shining in the sun, see the winding steps carved into the rock leading to the pool and boathouse. And when she turned her head, there were the mountains of Albania, tawny gold on the far horizon.

Sometimes Julian swam with her, Judy too, although neither of them swam as far or as strongly as Jane. Anthea only dipped into the water, usually in the pool, and preferred to lie in the sun, indolent as a cat, her skin sleek and brown against the white bikini she wore.

Sometimes in the late afternoon Jane walked in the olive groves at the back of the Villa, Judy invariably at her side. She had attached herself to Jane, and together they visited Chiron, Judy's small donkey, which was tethered there. They would often take him on the walk with them, Judy riding him from time to time, at others Jane leading him along, while Judy skipped about, picking wild flowers, singing and talking to herself in the happiest way.

One day they came upon a woman walking through the grove with a plump ewe tied to a length of string, while following her came two tiny lambs. They were the most beguiling of creatures, their faces patched with black and white fur as soft as satin. The woman, simply dressed in a voluminous cotton skirt and top with a white cotton headdress crowning her seamed brown face and hiding her hair, said a few words in Greek and then lifted one of the lambs and placed it in Judy's arms where it lay, its cottonwool legs dangling helplessly against her. Judy was ecstatic, her small face beamed with delight as she cradled the tiny body to her and crooned to it.

Another day they encountered a bent old man wandering among the irrigation ditches which bisected the fields beneath the olive trees. He carried a basket over one arm and held a knotted stick in the other with which he poked about in the long grass. When he saw Jane and Judy watching him he gave them a toothless grin and then, after a few moments, called out to them. As they walked up to him he held out one hand in which was a large squirming tortoise. He put it down on the grass, pushing the piece of over-ripe tomato, with which he had obviously enticed it, along the ground, but the tortoise, bent upon escape, went scrambling away to hide itself again.

Poor tortoise, Jane thought, wondering what its ultimate fate would be, and in an effort to avoid any sad end, she managed to convey to the old man that she would buy the tortoise from him. A few drachmas changed hands and Judy, highly delighted, wrapped the tortoise up in Jane's cardigan for want of anything better and in turn they carried the puzzled reptile back to the Villa Tyche, where it soon found a sheltered corner in the rockery.

There was always something fresh to see in the woods. The small single-storeyed buildings in their tiny garden, scattered here and there under the olive trees, fascinated Jane. One day outside such a homestead she counted one horse, three cows, five sheep, two donkeys, two goats, several hens, three cats and a dog. That was the animal contingent. The human one consisted of an old man who looked like the grandfather, busy with a wheelbarrow of stones he was carting away. A younger man was repairing a small hand tractor. As he did so a woman came out of the house to hang out a string of washing, followed by two small girls playing about on the dusty earth, and even as Jane stood watching, a boy of about fifteen arrived on a motor bike.

Jane, who had not seen this form of peasant economy before, thought as she turned away that she had never seen people who seemed to lead such self-supporting lives.

The name of the Villa intrigued her too.

'It's very unusual,' she said one day to Julian. 'Does it mean anything special?'

'Tyche was said to be the daughter of Zeus,' he told her in answer. 'She was goddess of good luck, giving or denying gifts usually without reason. I believe the Romans, with whom she was more popular than the Greeks, portrayed her juggling with a ball. This was meant to convey the instability of fortune.' He smiled wryly. 'It's certainly the way she has acted for us—everything coming our way and then a run of bad times.'

Jane, seeing the evidence of money in the setting and furnishings of the Villa Tyche, the two cars, Anthea's expensive clothes, found Julian's implication hard to believe.

Perhaps he was referring to the breakdown of his health? That was certainly bad luck. But perhaps, from what Vance had said, brought about by Julian's efforts to acquire such material benefits?

The next morning Anthea surprised Jane by saying,

'I have instructions from Julian to take you on a sight-seeing tour. Where would you like to go? To Corfu and perhaps a look round the Achilleon?'

Jane hesitated, not sure if Anthea really wanted to take her, or whether it would be just a chore imposed upon her by Julian.

'I would enjoy going very much, but are you sure I'm not being a nuisance?'

'Not at all. You've been awfully good amusing Judy. She can be a little pest at times.'

Jane had already seen enough of Corfu town to be charmed by it; by the elegant Regency palace, now a museum, which dominated the main square, and by the park with its many trees and statues. Here too was the famous cricket ground, a legacy of fifty years of British occupation, and a delightfully ornamental bandstand.

Anthea took Jane through the narrow streets where pink and yellow houses crowded against the shops and alleyways hung with lines of washing, interspersed now and again with some gem of Venetian architecture. They visited the Church of St. Spiridon, the patron saint of the island, and Anthea pointed out to Jane the Doxaras paintings on the ceiling and the handsome wrought iron screen of the gallery.

After this she suggested they went to one of the cafés situated in the long arcade facing the cricket ground and the old Fortress and have coffee and a snack lunch before going on to the Achilleon.

Here, where once only the nobility of Corfu were allowed to stroll, had been built an imitation of the Rue de Rivoli by the French at the end of the late eighteenth century. Now it seemed to Jane as if the entire population of Corfu town wandered there during the course of the day, not to mention American, German, Italian, British and Greek tourists.

The drive to the Achilleon Palace was up a steep winding road through small hamlets, past tall villas which must once have been beautiful in the grand Venetian style, but which now looked shabby and forgotten. There were vast woods, pine and poplar and oak trees growing in profusion mixed with tall cypress and all set against a background of mountains receding into blue distances.

The Achilleon Palace seemed an empty echoing place striving to achieve a grandeur entirely at variance with the charm and simplicity of the island. A marble staircase led up to a mirrored wall which reflected the hall below. Here it divided and went up on either side to the rooms now used as a casino. The most interesting part of the palace to Jane was the room on the ground floor where the few souvenirs of the unhappy Elizabeth of Austria were displayed, and her face, in all its haunting beauty, stared out at one from the several photographs. The private chapel next door to this was more rewarding, especially the glorious blue of the Della Robbia marble frescoes.

'The gardens and the views are the best part of the Achilleon,' Anthea said, as she and Jane walked up the winding steps to the terraces overlooking the bay. She gestured. 'See.'

Jane walked to the stone balustrade and stared down at the green forests falling away beneath, at the shimmering blue sea far below, and beyond this, the mountains of Albania, purple and amethyst and silver in the sun. The coastline curved away on either side, mountainous and magnificent; grey-green with olive and myrtle trees. It was this density of growth which gave Corfu its unique beauty, Jane thought, the richness and the sense of unchanging peace. It must have been the view of the bay of Gastouri that had captured the tragic Empress and caused her to build the Achilleon on this exact spot, as if so doing she would find a serenity of spirit to match her surroundings.

'She never did, of course,' Anthea said, in answer to Jane's remark on the subject. 'She came here for a few years and stayed from time to time and then she went away for good.'

Jane glanced down at the guide book in her hand.

'It says here it was after the unveiling of the memorial statue to her dead son that she left and never came back.'

They had come to the statue of Elizabeth herself, which stood gazing out over the bay to the distant mountains, the face pensive and remote.

'She looks very sad,' Jane said.

'She wasn't only sad—I'm sure she was mad. Not seriously, like her cousin Ludwig of Bavaria, but slightly. Certainly she was neurotic and unbalanced, and very egotistical. I always felt a bit sorry for poor old Franz Josef, but of course, he was the wrong man for her.' Anthea lifted her slim shoulders in a shrug. 'She should never have married him.'

'Wasn't she in love with someone else—some Englishman?' Jane asked.

'I doubt it. She was supposed to have had lovers, but I don't think she loved anyone but herself. She was searching for someone—something. My own theory is she was probably frigid.' Anthea turned away. 'Shall we go on and see the rest of the gardens?'

The growth was lush everywhere, even in late October. Roses, jasmines, vines, oleanders, hibiscus, bougainvillea—grew in profusion. An enormous date palm was in flower, something Jane had never seen before. A small curving balcony gave on to yet another view over the grove of trees; zinnias and petunias and delicate pink geraniums were set about a marble seat, a lantern hung overhead. It was a romantic spot. Jane could imagine sitting here some summer night with the garden lit by the torches held aloft in the hands of the statues, while the moon turned the sea to silver and the wind sighed in the forest trees below.

It was time to return to the Villa.

'Thank you for showing me so much,' Jane said as they drove homewards. 'It's been fascinating.'

'No trouble,' Anthea said carelessly. 'We might go to the north coast when Vance gets back—it's really the most beautiful part.'

'I'd love that. It would be nice to see more of the island before I—before we leave.'

She felt Anthea's quick sideways glance on her.

'I suppose you're going back to Rome with Vance?'

'Yes, I—yes, I think so.' Would she go back to Rome—and if she did, would she see Gino again? What was happening to him now? Perhaps he had fallen in love with Francesca and was entirely happy about his future marriage. Yet she could not bear to think he had forgotten her.

Anthea's voice broke in on her shadowed thoughts.

'Do tell me how and where you met Vance. It all sounds so romantic—love at first sight.' She shrugged. 'It never happened to me. I'd known Julian for years and years.'

Jane bit her lip, wondering what to say, what explanation to give. Supposing when Vance returned Anthea asked him the same question? She decided she must stick as near to the truth as possible.

'We met on a—on a tour. I mean, I was showing a party round the Piazza Navona and—and Vance was there. He sort of—joined in with us. He spoke to me. That's how we—we met.'

'*Really?* It doesn't sound a bit like Vance. You mean, that was it? You spoke to one another and—*wham*!' The green eyes slid round to Jane again, taking in the long brown hair blowing free in the wind, the pink striped cotton shirt and V-neck sweater over not-so-new pink terylene pants. 'It's incredible! Oh, please don't think I'm being rude, but the whole thing sounds like a rather corny film. Vance is so sophisticated—one hardly expects him to fall fathoms deep in love at the drop of a hat.' She turned her gaze back to the road ahead before adding, 'And—if you'll forgive my saying so—you don't even appear to be his type.'

Jane felt a rising resentment at the almost insolent tone of Anthea's voice. But she answered calmly enough, 'Has he a type? I didn't realise.'

Anthea's mouth thinned.

'He—admires a certain sort of girl, yes. I do know that.'

'And I'm not it?' Jane enquired coolly. 'Well, it doesn't seem to matter, does it? He—we're engaged.'

She was glad that they had reached the turning for the Villa. She didn't want to sound rude or ungracious. Anthea had been kind and given her a happy day, and she must not allow the implied criticism to rile her.

As the car slid to a standstill she put her hand to the door, and making her voice sound as pleasant as possible, said,

'Thank you again for such a nice day. I have enjoyed it.'

Anthea gave no answer but a slight shrug, and at that moment Judy came running out to greet them.

'Mummy—hello, Mummy! Have you had a nice day? I wish I could have come too.' She threw herself against Anthea and hugged her round the knees.

Anthea laid one hand absently on the dark curls.

'Careful, poppet—you'll crease my dress. Oh, I'm so *hot*, and quite exhausted. I must have a long lovely drink.'

She moved away with Judy clinging to one hand, leaving Jane feeling that after all she had been a nuisance. As she walked slowly after them into the cool tiled hall she heard Judy say,

'Uncle Vance is here—he came this afternoon.'

For a moment Jane was arrested in her tracks. Vance back again. She had a sudden remembrance of him, of their last meeting, his dark unsmiling face and cold voice, and she felt a sense of trepidation at the thought of their next encounter. Then she squared her shoulders and moved on.

How absurd. She wasn't frightened of him.

She heard Anthea's voice, warm and welcoming, say, 'Vance! What a lovely surprise. When did you get back?'

Jane didn't hear his reply. As she stood irresolute, a shadow darkened the open doorway—immensely tall, formidable. Before she could move she felt two arms seize hold of her, felt herself caught up in a close embrace and the next second Vance's mouth came down on hers in a passionate kiss.

CHAPTER NINE

AT first Jane was too stupefied by the suddenness of it all to speak or protest. And in any case, held tight in Vance's arms, her lips crushed under his, it was hardly possible to do anything but submit to his embrace. After a moment rationality returned and she made an effort to free herself, bringing both hands up against his broad chest in an attempt to push him away. But the more she struggled the more suffocating became his hold, and then, moving his mouth a fraction away from hers, he whispered in a low fierce voice,

'For God's sake, put a little realism into the act! You're supposed to be my loving fiancée welcoming me back again. Don't push me away—put your arms round my neck and look as if you mean business.'

Jane was so stunned she found herself obeying mechanically, leaning closer into Vance's hold, lifting her arms to link them behind his neck. And as she felt his lips take hers again she no longer resisted but, in the most inexplicable way, felt herself responding to his kiss. She couldn't understand it. One moment she had been indignant, outraged, the next she was being carried away on an almost swooning tide of emotion. When at last Vance released her she felt quite giddy and had to cling to him for support. A moment after she collected herself and moved away, brushing back the hair from her hot forehead.

She became aware of Anthea and Julian standing below the steps of the archway, witness of Vance's torrid greeting. Her eyes met Anthea's and she was startled by the coldness of her ice-green glance. Then she heard Vance's voice behind her saying,

'Come and tell me what you've been doing while I was away.'

112

Jane walked ahead of him down the steps into the living-room, aware of a confusion of feeling as she did so. To be kissed like that! More particularly, to respond to such love-making. To—to even *like* it. No, of course she hadn't *liked* it. How could she? She was still in love with Gino and Vance meant nothing to her. Yet there had been something exciting, overwhelming in that kiss, in the closeness of his tigerish embrace.

Vance's fingers touched her arm.

'Let's go on to the terrace,' and they moved out of the room away from the other two. She heard Judy's voice say something and Julian answer, 'No, come here, poppet. Uncle Vance wants to talk to Jane,' before she and Vance were out of earshot at the far end of the terrace.

Jane was too self-conscious to start any conversation. She stood leaning against the balustrade staring at the sea, mirror-smooth, deep dark blue in the late afternoon sun-shine, and said nothing, because she could think of nothing to say. Without turning her head to look, she was aware that Vance had come to stand alongside her, and out of the corner of her eye saw one well-shaped brown hand resting on the stonework within a few inches of her own.

He broke the silence to say, 'You did very well. Quite a promising pupil.'

His voice was mocking, but she refused to look at him.

'Th-thank you.'

'If I didn't know better I'd think you'd almost enjoyed it.'

She stared determinedly at a small caique on the water below, its red sail and gaily striped paintwork making a splash of colour on the shining sea.

'You asked for a realistic effort.'

'Most certainly. I'm sure we fooled Julian and'—he hesi-tated a moment—'and Anthea, very nicely.' He moved his hand from the wall and the next second Jane felt his fingers under her chin as he turned her face round so that she was forced to look at him.

113

'What's the matter? You've not gone all shy on me, have you?'

Jane took a deep breath, very aware of his nearness, of the intent stare of the grey eyes behind the thick black lashes.

'Of course not. I—it's all part of—the act, as you call it. I'm glad you think I was—adequate.'

Now he smiled, the infrequent smile that altered his face so completely, taking the frowning sternness from it and leaving his expression gentle yet still a trifle mocking.

'Adequate is an—inadequate word. You were—what's the expression—fab? Fantastic? Anyway, I confess, whatever you thought about *my* performance, I enjoyed *yours*.'

Jane felt the colour come in her cheek. She longed to look away but was riveted, motionless, like some hypnotised rabbit under Vance's magnetic dark gaze.

He whistled softly. 'You're blushing! Heavens, I didn't think there was a girl left who could do that in this day and age.' He let his hand fall from her chin and said lightly, 'I didn't mean to embarrass you.' He took her hand in his and pulled her gently round towards one of the cane chairs. 'Sit down there and I'll fetch some drinks and then we'll talk about the things you've done this week and about the things I've been doing. What would you like? Gin—sherry—ouzo?'

He was the most disconcerting person Jane had ever met. One moment domineering, formidable, the next kind and companionable. She sank down into the cane lounger and said stammeringly,

'Ouzo, I think. Th-thank you.'

When he had gone she put a hand to her burning cheek. Her fingers touched the side of her face where Vance had laid his fingers. The skin seemed to still tingle from the remembrance of it.

He came back with glasses on a small tray and two letters.

114

'Some mail for you—both from England, by the look of them.'

Jane took them from his outstretched hand.

'Thank you.' She glanced down at the two envelopes. 'One's from my sister and the other from the girl I worked with in Rome.' She laid them on her lap and added, with an upward glance. 'I sent them my change of address.'

To her surprise he was frowning again.

'Have you written to Rome too—doing the same?'

'To Rome?'

'To your Italian friend. Does he know where you are?' His voice was impatient.

'Of course not.' Her voice echoed the impatience in his. 'Though really, what business is it of yours?'

He shrugged.

'One never knows. You might be just silly enough to be in touch. Better leave well alone.'

She said stiffly, ironically, 'Thank you.'

There was a silence, then he said, with a shrug,

'I'm sorry. Tell me what you've been doing in my absence.'

She took the cue from him.

'Anthea very kindly took me to Corfu one day, and we saw a lot of the town. Also the Achilleon. I thought that most interesting because of its associations, and the gardens and views are beautiful.'

'Yes. What about the countryside—did you explore it?'

She shook her head.

'No. Julian offered me the use of one of the cars, but I haven't taken him up on that yet.'

'You *must* see some of the beauty spots—Paleocastritsa and Kalami and Ayios Giordis—half a dozen others.' He smiled briefly, 'What have we been doing, cooping you up here? The fact is, before I left for Milan I was flat out working on the details for this merger.'

'How—how did your business affairs go? Were you successful?'

He shrugged again.

'Reasonably so, I think. At least I've done the ground work for Julian—he would never have been up to all the running around and the endless discussions. But I'm far from being the Big Tycoon type.'

'Have you much more work to do?'

'More than I could wish for. But it's what I came here to do.'

Jane glanced at him and hesitated. Then putting down the glass in her hand she said slowly,

'Could I be of any use, d'you think? I'm a competent typist—and I can also take down shorthand.' She smiled. 'Not very quickly, I'm afraid.'

Vance had been staring into space, his face dark and frowning. For a moment Jane thought he had not heard her suggestion, then he jerked his head round and said,

'Sorry—what did you say?'

She repeated her remarks and saw his face relax slightly.

'That would be a help. It's these damnable figures—and the endless specifications, half of them in Italian. I never thought to ask you—and of course, you were handicapped with the use of only one hand. We might have a try-out tomorrow morning and see if you can manage some of the work. I would be grateful.'

'I'd like that,' Jane said. She gestured towards the green mountains and the shining bay. 'I'd feel then I was earning some of this.'

He said stiffly, 'You're earning it acting as my fiancée— remember?'

She wanted to say, 'But *why*? Why this absurd pretence? I don't understand. It seems so unnecessary,' but something in his remote expression checked her. Instead, she stood up, saying,

'Would you excuse me, I'd like to wash before dinner and—and read my letters.'

He was already on his feet.

'I'm sorry. Of course—go ahead. I've things to see to

116

myself.'

In the bedroom, changing her dress and brushing out her long brown hair, Jane thought again of Vance and of his abrupt change of mood. He was certainly a mystery man. She would never begin to understand the reason why he had brought her to the Villa Tyche. Except that in some way it was connected with Anthea and Julian. She frowned into the mirror, puzzling over it all, thinking that whereas Julian seemed pleased about her supposed engagement to Vance, Anthea appeared to resent the fact, and she was at little pains to conceal her surprise that Vance should ever have fallen in love with someone as young and unsophisticated as Jane.

She shrugged, putting down the hairbrush to pick up the letters which had come from England to re-read them.

Rosemary's letter was full of family news. The children were well, Bill was working hard; it had been a good year for the Victoria plums and she had bottled pounds and made jam. How lovely for Jane going to Corfu—what sort of a job had she got there? She was glad Jane had liked Italy so much—she deserved the break.

Meg was surprised at Jane's sudden change of address. 'You dog,' she wrote. 'What happened? I thought you were all set with that super job in Rome. Not to mention Gino. Have you had a row or something? I can't wait to hear all the details.' She went on to say that she was working at the London Agency until Christmas and her wedding to Tony. 'Can you make it if I send you an invitation? If you're not tied up with Gino, please try. Corfu sounds gorgeous, but what exactly are you *doing* there? Some sort of au pair?'

Jane smiled, thinking that Meg's letter was so like her, full of a lively interest in Jane's affairs and a happy exuberance.

The rest of the evening passed pleasantly enough. Hestia served a late dinner consisting of fish cooked in delicious red pepper sauce and *sofrito*, steak served with a rich brown

117

gravy, and then *paklava*, layers of a leaf-like pastry covering an ambrosial mixture of honey and nuts.

'Tomorrow I shall get down to work again,' Vance said as they sat over coffee. 'Jane is kindly going to type out some of the stuff I have brought back from Milan and then, Julian, you and I can go through it all together.'

Anthea turned a cool green gaze on Jane.

'So you can type, too. How clever and useful!'

'Very useful,' Vance said. 'It means we can get through the work that much quicker.'

Anthea looked round at him. She said gently, 'You sound as if you want to get away from here in a hurry. Do you?'

For a moment Vance didn't answer. His glance was dark and moody on Anthea's beautiful face. Then he said abruptly,

'I came here to help Julian—you know that.'

'Of course. But do you have to make it sound such a chore? As if seeing'—she hesitated before adding with delicate emphasis—'*us* again is of little pleasure to you. After all, we are your family, Vance. You've no one else.'

Still with that dark frowning look, Vance said,

'I have Jane now.' He reached for Jane's hand. 'Haven't I, Jane?'

His sudden grip on her fingers caused Jane to wince. She said stammeringly, 'Y-yes.'

Julian leaned forward.

'I think Jane is the best thing that's happened to Vance in years. I told her so when we first met. She's ready to settle down with him, she wants children, she's a capable little thing and, I may add, damn pretty with it all.' He smiled at Jane before adding, 'I hope you know how lucky you are, Vance.'

Vance inclined his head.

'Oh, indeed.' His voice was ironic as he turned his glance on Jane. 'It's comforting to know she has these domestic and material qualities.'

Jane coloured, very much aware of that phrase 'she wants

118

children' echoing on the air. She was relieved when Vance, still retaining hold of her hand, said,

'If no one minds, I'm going to turn in. It's been a long day and there's a pile of work to be got through to-morrow. What about you, Jane? Coming to say goodnight to me?'

She allowed herself to be pulled to her feet.

'Yes. I—of course.'

Julian smiled up at them. 'All right, love birds. Clear off—we don't mind. Goodnight, Vance. 'Night, Jane.'

Anthea's face was a lovely mask, smiling but without warmth. 'Goodnight.'

Jane walked ahead of Vance into the living-room and up the shallow steps to the hall. It was absurd, but her knees seemed to be trembling, as if she thought Vance was going to repeat the performance of the ardent lover. Hardly. The audience had been left behind on the terrace. When he paused by the door of the study she had a brief idea that he might insist upon a session there for appearances' sake, as before. But all he said was,

'Goodnight, Jane. See you in the morning.'

'Oh. Yes. Goodnight.' He turned the door handle and went into the room, leaving her to go on up the stairs.

How unpredictable he was, she thought as she started to undress. Unpredictable and puzzling.

The whole of the next morning Jane worked with Vance in the study, taking down letters, going through figures and statements with him, typing out details of the memorandum and Articles of Association connected with the merger of the two companies. It was a concentrated effort on the part of both of them and it was one o'clock before Vance pushed aside the papers on his desk and said, with a sigh of relief,

'That's enough for today. Jane, you're a wonderful girl. Julian's right. I think we shall have to keep you in the family, if only as a business asset. Come on, you deserve a drink and this afternoon we'll go along the coast road so you can see it and perhaps swim somewhere.'

She smiled. 'That would be fun.'

For the next few days Jane and Vance lived to a pattern. In the mornings they worked together over the papers and figures, and in the afternoons Vance took Jane out in the car. For the first time she really saw the island and its legendary beauty. Ayios Giordis with its smooth sandy beach surrounded by rocky hills and vineyards. Along the east road to Dassia, past the sophisticated build-up of modern hotels and bungalows of Nissaki, a small creek of gloriously blue water, and Kalami, the beautiful bay where the White House, once home of Lawrence Durrell, stood and where he had written *Prospero's Cell*. South to the olive groves of Moraitka and the lake of Korisson and its miles and miles of paradisical sandy beaches, completely deserted and unspoilt.

Palaeocastritsa was a full day's outing. 'We shall play hookey today,' Vance announced as he selected a bottle of wine to put in the picnic basket.

Anthea watched him, her green eyes glittering between dark lashes.

'I suppose your plans don't include other people—Julian and me, for instance? It might be rather nice to take us along too. But perhaps we should be intruding on your romantic isolation?'

'You suppose rightly,' Vance said. His voice was cool and impersonal. 'However, tomorrow we plan to take the boat to Mouse Island—Jane hasn't seen it yet, so shall we make it a family party?'

'If you're sure you could bear not being alone together,' Anthea said edgily.

For the first time Vance looked at her.

'All lovers are selfish enough to wish to exclude the world. Don't you remember that you felt the same way?'

Anthea met his dark glance and for a moment they stared at one another, then she looked away.

'Yes, I remember. I remember that I wanted only to be with——' she stopped abruptly, and Jane, who had been a

120

witness to the small altercation, stared in puzzlement at them both. She had the oddest feeling that Anthea had been about to say some other name than Julian's and that was why she had hesitated.

Vance pushed the bottle of wine into the basket and turned to Jane.

'Time to get moving, Jane. We want to enjoy the best of the day—it soon gets dark.'

The drive to Paleocastritsa went along the east coast some way, then branched off towards the north. The road was a fine one, built, so Vance told her, by British soldiers during the occupation of the island in the nineteenth century. There were magnificent views across forests of pine and fir and larch and cypress to Mount Pantocrator, the highest mountain in the island, with its monastery built near the summit. Soon the road started to climb, winding steeply through the olive groves and vineyards where black-clad women were working. There were cows and sheep under the trees, a billy goat with an enormous beard looked over the wall at them, his jaws moving rhythmically.

As the road opened up Jane saw wooded vistas and curving bays of peacock blue and emerald green glittering in the sun.

'Oh, it's fabulous!' she gasped.

Vance turned his head. This morning he had returned to his former moody silence, and Jane had taken her cue and spoken little during the drive.

'Yes, it's beautiful all right.'

'You—you're awfully kind, going to so much trouble to show me everything.'

He shrugged. 'The least I can do. You might as well see it all while you're here.'

There was something ominous about that last phrase, 'While you're here.' As if she would not come again to Corfu. But why should she not? It was just the sort of place she would wish to return to. Yet she had a curious sinking of heart at the thought that it was most unlikely she would ever be there again with Vance.

They reached Lakones at last, a small town on the top of the mountain. It consisted of little more than a long narrow street with houses set here and there against the hillside. Vance parked the car and suggested they walk round and then stop for a drink at the *taverna* overlooking the bay.

The houses opened directly on to the roadway and showed simply furnished interiors, yet often with charming china and silver ornaments. On the steps of one house were a pair of handsome cockerels wearing red worry beads round their necks. At the foot of a steep cobbled lane was an ancient church with twin belfrys and a grassy graveyard. It was all fascinating to Jane and she was almost sorry when Vance directed their footsteps back to the *taverna*.

Here, over glasses of sharp-tasting retsina and with black olives to nibble, they looked down at Paleocastritsa and the ruined Byzantine fortress of Castellos Angelos set on its hill beyond the beach. Then it was time to return to the car and drive slowly down the steep road to the bay below.

It was warm enough to swim in the pellucid sea; to float on clear aquamarine water, gazing back at the wooded heights which rose on either side of the cove, enclosing it in a small sunlit world. And afterwards there was the al fresco meal, warmed by the wine Vance had brought with them.

'I suppose we should have gone to the restaurant back there and had one of those famous lobster lunches. But I wasn't sure where we would get to for lunch.' He glanced up at the sky. 'The weather's on the change—it might not have been warm enough to swim.'

Jane's glance followed his.

'It looks perfect—hardly a cloud in the sky.'

He shrugged, lifting a chicken leg to his mouth.

'It's my bet the rains are coming.'

'Then it's all to the good that we're having a picnic now, while it lasts,' Jane said.

They had both dressed after the swim, slipping into slacks and sweaters. Now, the meal over, Vance stretched out a few yards away and closed his eyes, his profile remote and stern as that on some crusader's tomb, black lashes casting a shadow on high cheekbones.

Jane didn't sleep. She pillowed her head on her arms and stared up at the blue dome of the sky. The radiance of the golden day lay like an aura over the land, a sunlit ambience, peaceful and serene. It was part of the island's magic, this tranquillity and sense of contentment that came, like a spell, to soothe one.

Yet today Jane was not content. An awareness of melancholy cast a shadow across the shining day and when she tried to pin down the sensation, to discover its origin, she found that in some way, it had to do with Vance.

CHAPTER TEN

VANCE had been right about the weather. During the night Jane woke to hear the rattle of the wind through the dusty leaves of the fig trees near her window—a harsh staccato sound like the echo of a myriad feet pattering by. Next morning there were clouds in the sky and a fresh sea running.

'It's not very inviting to go on the boat,' Anthea said frowningly. 'Why don't we go somewhere in the car instead?'

'Jane and I have our stint of work to do first,' Vance explained. 'If we go on the boat it's only for an hour or so this afternoon.'

'You were out all day yesterday,' said Anthea. 'Can't you give up another to be with Julian and me? Besides, if the weather is going to break as it looks like doing, Jane won't see much more of the place in sunshine.'

Vance shrugged. 'That's an argument. All right, we'll go off again. Any suggestions?'

'What about Sidari?' queried Julian. 'Those curiously formed cliffs should intrigue Jane. If you haven't been there already, that is.'

'No, we haven't. It's not a very good road from Kastellanoi, but there's a restaurant where we can get some sort of lunch. Sidari it is.'

'Shall we be able to swim again?' Jane asked.

'Possibly. The water will be warm even if the wind is cool. Take your things anyway,' said Vance.

Today they were going in Anthea's Triumph and she had elected to drive, at least to begin with, and with a smiling gesture, beckoned Vance to sit in the front beside her, leaving Jane and Julian to sit together at the back. To begin with the road took the same direction as the day before,

124

running along Corfu harbour towards Gouvia and then taking the Skipero road instead of branching westwards for Paleocastritsa as before.

It was windy—the olive trees rippled like a grey-green sea and the tall black cypress bowed and swayed under the jostling breeze, dusty leaves blew about the pattering hooves of the occasional donkey trotting along the empty road, while across the pale sky fluffy white clouds moved swiftly before the wind.

Julian, who was invariably talkative, rattled away non-stop as they drove along. Jane found him a puzzling person; although he seemed gay and extrovert there were times when he lapsed into quietness. His moods held none of the frowning darkness of Vance's, but were more those of restlessness and uncertainty, as if he suffered from an inner tension. Perhaps it had to do with his illness, Jane thought, the nervous breakdown Vance had told her of. She had a feeling of sympathy towards Julian and could not help but like him.

At the front of the car Anthea's lovely face turned constantly towards Vance as she too, it appeared, kept up a steady conversation. Jane couldn't hear her voice nor Vance's replies, but she was aware that his answers were brief, that the clean-cut profile turned unsmilingly to look at Anthea before his erect dark head stared back to the road ahead.

The last part of the drive was over a secondary road and the car had to go slowly over some of the broken and uneven surface. When they finally reached Sidari Jane saw that it was little more than a cluster of houses and a sandy beach that seemed to stretch for miles. Out of the sea rose strange cliffs of sandstone, carved into peculiar shapes by the constant beat of the waves.

'How strange it is,' Jane said as they left the car and walked on to the shore. She gestured. 'I should like to swim through that opening.'

'Would you?' Vance gave her a cryptic smile. 'Do you

125

know, it's called the Canal d'Amour? If two people kiss in it the legend says they will live in harmony for ever.'

'Then *you* must both swim through it,' Julian stated smilingly. 'Just to make sure you qualify for the Dunmow Flitch.'

'I shouldn't think any of us will want to swim here to-day,' Anthea said sharply. 'The sea's quite rough and dreary-looking,' she shivered. 'Not to mention cold.'

Vance shook his head. He was staring at the rocks and did not look at her.

'It won't be cold. The thing is not to hang around afterwards. What about it, Julian? You coming?'

Julian hesitated.

'Might as well, I suppose. If the weather's breaking up this may be the last swim of the season. Come on, Anthea, take a chance. It will give you an appetite for lunch.'

She shrugged.

'I can't imagine what fun we're going to have out of it—but if you all insist, I suppose I shall have to join in.'

The sea was warm, the shallow waves bubbling over the stones. Anthea appeared in a scarlet mesh bikini which set off her sinuous figure and smooth tan to perfection. As the four of them waded in she appeared to stumble over a stone and clung on to Vance's arm for support. They made a striking pair, Vance tall and teak brown of body, powerful shoulder muscles rippling as he bent to hold Anthea out of the water. Jane looked and then looked away, while Julian, tanned too with the sun but painfully thin, stared at his wife and brother through narrowed eyes, before plunging into the deeper waves to swim away.

Jane followed him and soon they had swum beyond the rocks and were looking back at the curious formations, shaped like huge heads of strange animals. She caught sight of the splash of red that was Anthea, still close to the shore and the tall figure of Vance nearby. Julian came alongside Jane, puffing in a breast-stroke, already looking exhausted with swimming against the strong sea.

126

'I'm going back, Jane,' he gasped. 'Don't go too far out on your own.'

'No, I won't!' She watched his head go bobbing through the waves towards the shore and turned herself to float and rest. The water was wonderfully invigorating today, cool and fresh to the skin the further out one went.

After a few moments she saw a dark head coming towards her, two brown arms, flailing through the waves. *Vance.* On an impulse Jane couldn't account for, she began to swim in the opposite direction, towards the rocks and the opening between them. She knew quite well that he had only left Anthea to come in search of her for the look of the thing. To keep up the appearance of the devoted fiancé. Well, she wouldn't stay for him, she would go back to Julian.

A strong current was running against her, but Jane drove herself on and out of Vance's path and at last reached the fissure between the cliffs, the so-called Canal d'Amour. She headed into it and suddenly, without warning, one of the waves rushing through caught her head on and threw her sideways, banging her leg against the rock. She gasped in sudden pain, for the leg was the one previously injured in the car smash. Involuntarily, she swallowed mouthfuls of sea water and choking for air, sank down. As she surfaced, another wave drove her once more on to the side of the rock and this time the pain in her leg was agonising. For a moment Jane thought she was going to faint; blackness came before her eyes, water roared in her ears, she began to sink again. Then two arms caught hold of her and held her fast and a voice said,

'For heaven's sake, what are you up to?'

Jane couldn't speak, only cough and choke for breath against Vance's broad shoulders.

Unaware of the injury to her leg, he added,

'You're in no danger of drowning—I doubt if it's six foot deep here.'

Still she couldn't speak from the excruciating pain in her

leg, only staring helplessly up at him out of sea-drenched eyes.

He said, 'What's the matter? You look so—so imploring.' He bent his wet black head and brushed her mouth with his. 'There! Is that what you were waiting for? Now we shall never argue again but live amicably for ever.' As another tempestuous wave dashed towards them he said, 'Better swim out of here,' and turned her round. In so doing, Jane's injured leg knocked against his. Although Vance was not exactly rock-like, the muscular hardness of thigh and knee were such as to cause a fresh wave of pain through Jane's entire leg and this time, with not more than a slight gasp, she fainted away.

She came to, aware that she was in Vance's arms and being carried through the ebbing waves to the shore. Aware too of being laid gently down on the sand and of Vance bending over her to brush back the tangle of wet hair from her face. He chafed her hands in his own two, and started to rub her body, then he broke off with a sharp exclamation and Jane heard him say, 'Heavens, look at this leg!'

Julian's voice answered and Anthea said something, but Jane scarcely heard them through the misty darkness that came and went. After a moment or two the cloud cleared and she felt better. Vance's arm came round her to support her into a sitting position and leaning against his wet shoulder, she said feebly,

'I'm—sorry. Sorry—to be a—nuisance.'

Vance's deep voice said soothingly,

'Just hang on to me. Julian's going to wipe your leg. I'm afraid that old wound has broken open—you must have knocked it.'

She bit her lip on the spasm of pain.

'Yes, the sea—threw me against the—rock.'

His hand was tight on hers.

'Poor old thing—you're really in the wars!'

The gentleness of his tone made Jane feel momentarily tearful, but she resolutely fought such passing weakness and managed an apology for a smile. A few moments later the wound had been cleansed with alcohol from the flask that Julian always carried in his car for emergencies, and a makeshift bandage made from Vance's clean handkerchief had been tied round her leg.

'Now we'll take you back to Corfu,' said Vance. 'I'll carry you to the car.'

'But your lunch—none of you have had anything to eat,' Jane protested. 'Please let's go to the *taverna*—I shall be perfectly all right. My leg feels easier already.' She looked at Vance, his brown chest and shoulders from which the sea water was pearling away, leaving a dusting of salt on bare skin. A cardigan had been thrown over her own shoulders for warmth against the wind—a large enfolding one which felt like Vance's. 'You must get dressed.'

'Yes. Anthea'll help you.' He swung her lightly up into his arms. 'No argument. First stop Corfu and Dr. Karalis's surgery.'

Anthea was waiting by the car, already dressed in sweater and slacks.

'Feeling better?' Her voice was kind but cool and her green eyes flickered from Jane to Vance as he deposited her gently on the back seat.

'Yes—yes, thank you. But I'm so sorry to spoil everyone's day.'

Anthea shrugged.

'It wasn't an awfully good idea of Julian's to come here anyway—it's often windy. Can I help you into your things?' She looked over her shoulder at Vance. 'Where are you going to get dressed?'

'Round the back—chuck me a towel, will you, please?'

Jane's teeth were chattering, more from shock than cold, as she pulled on slacks and sweater. She rubbed her long wet hair and combed it into some semblance of tidiness, helped in offhand fashion by Anthea. Julian was already dressed and when he came to the side of the car to ask, in kindly tones, how Jane now felt, Vance appeared from behind the car and said,

'Would you sit in front with Anthea and I'll get in here with Jane.'

It was oddly comforting to have Vance sitting next to her on the way back. Jane, who had been given a strong swig of brandy from Julian's flask, felt rather dopey, but she was very aware of the warm masculine presence beside her. Once Vance put a hand on her own and asked, 'How's the leg feel?'

'Fine, thank you. It—it's much easier.'

He smiled at her, eyes kinder than usual.

'Good. Just relax—we'll soon be at the doctor. I expect he'll give you an injection against infection.'

Jane remembered Dr. Karalis's charming old house from her visit there when he had removed the plaster from the fractured arm. She remembered Dr. Karalis too and his penetrating dark eyes and saturn...

Now he clicked his tongue commiseratingly as he examined the torn and bruised leg.

'Is pretty painful, I think. How did you come to do this?' He made a careful probe to remove hair-like splinters of rock from the deeply gashed wound.

Vance answered for her.

'Miss Roper was swimming between the rocks at Sadari and a wave dashed her into the side.'

One thick black eyebrow rose.

'Ah so?' the doctor smiled. 'You were in the Canal d'Amour with your fiancé here, no? I hope you'd been through the prescribed ritual before this unfortunate accident occurred?'

Again Vance answered for her.

'Of course we had followed the tradition.' He made no mention of the sequence of events.

'Then all should go well with you both,' Dr. Karalis remarked. 'And now, with this final injection, all should go well with your leg, Miss Roper. Just rest it for a day—two days. I will see you again at the end of one week. Yes?'

'Yes. Thank you very much,' Jane said.

Vance took her arm.

'I'll bring Miss Roper back to you. Thank you, Doctor,' and with a shaking of hands all round he and Jane took their leave.

Back at the Villa Tyche, Judy, who had been left in the care of Kestia, came running to greet them and was full of affectionate concern for Jane.

'How horrid! I'm glad I didn't go with you after all, though I wanted to. I might have hurt myself on the rocks too.'

'Very unlikely,' Anthea said, ruffling the dark curls. 'You wouldn't have gone swimming through the Canal d'Amour, like Uncle Vance and Jane.'

Judy savoured the words.

'Can-al d-d—what did you say, Mummy?'

'It's a French word for love,' Julian explained. 'It's a sort of cavern place which two people who love one another visit together. If they exchange a kiss there, they live happily ever after.'

Judy stared up at him.

'Like a fairytale? The prince and the princess *always* live happily ever after.' She turned to her mother for confirmation. 'Don't they Mummy?'

'Perhaps, but that's only in fairytales. Come along, poppet. Jane has to go to bed now and rest her bad leg. You can talk to her later.'

Jane didn't really want to go to bed and be waited upon, but she realised if she wanted her leg to heal quickly she must do so. Hestia brought her a supper tray and Judy came and perched on the end of the bed after her bath, looking rosy and cherubic in a pink and white sprigged nightdress.

Anthea came to take her away and enquired of Jane how she felt.

'My leg's much easier now since Dr. Karalis dressed it.' She smiled hesitantly up at Anthea. 'I'm really nothing but a fraud.'

Anthea smiled back, but her green eyes were cool and speculating.

'Don't worry about that. Though you do seem accident-prone—first Vance's car, now this. I hope the kiss was worth it.'

Jane scarcely remembered that brief salute. She had felt too faint and far away at the time, but nevertheless her cheeks coloured under Anthea's mocking look. She said as casually as possible,

'Oh, one does these things as—as tribute to folklore. Like throwing a coin in the Trevi Fountain.'

'So you'll return to Rome? Then do you expect to live "happily ever after", as Judy puts it, with Vance because of today?'

'That would be asking miracles of a legend, wouldn't it?' Jane said lightly.

Anthea shrugged.

'I can't answer that one, never having tested it out with Julian.' She put a hand on Judy's shoulder. 'Say goodnight to Jane. It's long past your bedtime.'

When she had gone Jane lay back, thinking how Vance had kissed her in that strange rocky passageway. She couldn't remember it very well, but she did remember the strength of his arms about her, and the way he had carried her, so lightly and easily, to the safety of the shore. She remembered too the gentleness of his hand, stroking back her hair. It was queer how it had registered through the clouds of unconsciousness.

As if to confound her the object of her thoughts appeared unexpectedly in the doorway, first tapping, then obeying her call to come in.

'Hello.' He walked over to her bedside. 'How are you feeling now?'

She couldn't quite meet his searching glance.

'M-much better, thank you. I—I told Anthea, I feel a fraud.'

He shook his head and sat down, straddling a small chair and leaning his arms along the back so that he was facing Jane.

'I wouldn't say that. Your leg was a hell of a mess. Poor Jane, no wonder you blacked out.' He paused, then added, 'I do apologise for putting on the Romeo act—I'd no idea you had injured yourself like that.'

She looked away.

'It—it didn't matter. I was—was too——'

He smiled, lifting a black eyebrow.

'Too far gone? I felt like a rapist!'

This time Jane smiled too, managing to meet his quizzical glance. Before she could answer he said,

'That's better. You looked so serious when I came in just now. Did you eat any supper?'

'Yes. Actually I was hungry.'

'Good. I've been worrying about you.'

'Please don't. There's no need to.'

'I'm not so sure. You're proving to be a problem child—I hope it's safe to leave you when I go off to Athens.'

She was aware of a curious sinking feeling.

'Oh. You're—going away again?"

'Yes. Tomorrow most probably. The mail was waiting for me when we got back and some queries have arisen. One of the men from the firm in Milan is flying to Greece—they have a subsidiary company in Athens. Julian and I thought the best thing was to meet him there and sort things out.'

'I see.'

'You'll be all right here, won't you, resting and taking things easy. Anthea will look after you.'

'Yes. Yes, of course.'

He stood up, looking taller than ever as he stared down at Jane.

'Look after yourself, then. Goodnight, Jane.'

'Goodnight, Vance. And—and thank you.'

He smiled, hesitated, then walked towards the door.

'Sleep well,' he said, and was gone.

If Anthea had been there, or Julian, he would have kissed me, Jane thought. For appearances' sake only, of course. Not meaning anything. Then why this unaccountable regret that neither Anthea nor Julian had been there? She shook her head, as if to chide herself, and slid a little further down the bed. She closed her eyes, aware of a sense of depression and a tendency to feel weepy. Really, Jane thought, what on earth's the matter with me?

She slept badly, and woke in the morning to a grey day of rain and strong winds. When Hestia appeared with the breakfast tray she shook her head mournfully and gave a mock shiver, saying, 'Is cold today. Today we light fires.'

Anthea came in later and after enquiring about Jane's leg added, 'Don't bother to get up. It's a vile day. I'm taking Julian and Vance to the airport—they want to get away as soon as possible.' She added carelessly, 'Have you plenty to read?'

'Yes, thank you—but I could get up. I feel so lazy lying here.'

'You can get up tomorrow. Your leg will be that much better. Judy wants to come up and see you—may she?'

'Oh, please. I'd love to have her with me.'

Judy came bounding in, bringing her favourite doll and a new book which she implored Jane to read to her. As Jane embarked upon the startling adventures of Sandy the Space Cat she wondered if Vance would come and see her again before he left. Just before midday, above the noise of the wind, she heard a car starting up and when Hestia came in to take Judy downstairs for her lunch she told Jane that Madame had taken Monsieur Morley and his brother to the airport.

It seemed an endless afternoon. Jane read and dozed and read again and thought of getting up after all, and while she was in a state of indecision Anthea returned and came in to see her to say that the plane had got off on time.

'I did some shopping in Corfu and had lunch with a friend at the hotel there. Have you been all right? You're in the best place, believe me.'

'I thought of getting up—I feel so idle.'

Anthea shrugged.

'Do as you wish. I'm going to shower and change—it's teeming with rain. They say once it starts at this time of the year it goes on for days—weeks even. I hope to heaven Vance and Julian don't stay away long—it will be too dreary for words, just you and I and Judy.'

When she had gone Jane started to get up. Her knee was stiff and painful, the wound in the leg throbbing afresh as she moved slowly round bathing and dressing. She put on a trouser suit and hobbled downstairs to find the welcome of a log fire burning in the huge stone fireplace. Judy was stretched out on the cream goatskin rug in front of it with Pookie, the Siamese cat, lying beside her, smoke-blue eyes staring unwinkingly at the rosy flames.

Just before dinner Anthea appeared in a caftan of striped wine and blue brocade, her dark hair loose about her shoulders.

'Let's have a drink to cheer ourselves up. What would you like, Jane? Gin, Dubonnet, sherry, Martini, ouzo?' At Jane's request for Martini she poured out a glass and helped herself to a liberal gin and french. Collapsing into one of the low armchairs, she lit a cigarette and through a cloud of smoke, said to Judy,

'Aren't you in bed yet? Where has Hestia got to?'

'I'm ready for bed,' Judy answered gravely, and smoothed the front of her pink dressing gown.

'Then it's time you were off! Say goodnight to Jane and give Mummy a kiss, and go and find Hestia.'

Judy looked back reproachfully from the doorway.

'When will Daddy be back?'

'As soon as possible, I hope,' Anthea replied. 'Now, scoot!'

Dinner was eaten to the accompaniment of a dull echo of thunder followed by the rattle of hailstones against the shutters and the lash of rain. The wind had risen and was screeching round the house and moaning through the trees, while, from time to time, Jane could hear the crash of the sea on the rocks below the villa.

Anthea shuddered.

'What a ghastly night! Thank goodness Julian and Vance got away before all this blew up.' She paced restlessly about the room, one moment switching on the radio, only to turn it off in exasperation at the bangs and crackles that emerged from it, the next moment flinging herself on to the settee or an armchair to flick through the pages of a magazine. A few moments later she would light a cigarette or attempt the crossword puzzle in the newspaper.

Once she stared at Jane and said,

'How on earth can you sit there so quietly? You can't possibly be reading that book. Talk to me—tell me about your job in Rome.' The green eyes narrowed. 'Tell me about you and Vance. When are you going to be married?'

'We—haven't settled on a date yet,' Jane answered hesitantly.

'You must have made *some* plans. Where you're going to live, for instance? Or does it all depend on whether Vance joins up with Julian? He ought to, you know. There's a lot of money to be made in Morleys—especially now, with this merger. You'll have to use your influence.'

Jane felt uncomfortable under Anthea's attack.

'I—Vance will make his own decision.'

Anthea's voice softened, she smiled at Jane with extraordinary sweetness.

'Forgive me. I'm not trying to interfere. You must remember I know Vance so well and it makes me sad to feel he and Julian are not as close as they used to be. If you marry Vance, we shall be practically sisters. Have you thought of that? So do let's be friends and allow me to advise you as much as I can.'

Jane stared blankly. *Sisters?* The mere idea was alarming; but of course, she must remember, it would never happen. She wasn't *really* going to marry Vance.

She said with difficulty,

'Th-thank you. I—appreciate your—your thought for me. But I doubt if I could influence Vance very much. He—he has a very decided mind.' She glanced at the clock and added hesitantly, 'I—I think if you'll excuse me I shall go to bed.' She stood up, leaning awkwardly on her good leg.

'Goodnight, Anthea.'

Anthea was still smiling, but somehow fixedly.

'You're a cagey little thing, aren't you? Not exactly the chatty kind. I suppose you think it's no business of mine. Goodnight, and sleep well.'

It was another stormy night. Jane lay awake for a long time listening to the wind and the boom of the sea before finally she fell asleep. The next day the wind was still in evidence and the rain sheeting down. Hestia brought Jane a breakfast tray and at Jane's remonstrance, shook her head and said, 'Madame also in bed.' Two dimples appeared in her round cheek—the black eyes smiled mischievously. 'She say nothings to get up for.'

Jane was down first that morning and in the living-room, sitting by the cheerful log fire writing a letter to Rosemary, when Anthea appeared, glamorous in cream jersey pants and a turtle-necked cream sweater.

'Hello, how's the leg?' She didn't wait for Jane's answer, but went to the big window and stared out frowningly. 'What a frightful prospect! Worse than ever.' She shuddered and came back to the fire. 'What on earth are we going to do with ourselves today?' She flung herself on to the settee and glanced round. 'Where's Judy?'

'She's in the kitchen. Hestia is making cakes—*kurabiedes*, I think she calls them.'

'Judy ought to be having her lessons. Julian or I usually see she has reading or writing. She goes to school next year.'

'Here, do you mean?'

'Heavens, I hope not. We won't want to be here *next*

137

winter. We shall be back in England—or perhaps living in Italy.' She looked at Jane. 'Perhaps we'll live in Rome—near you and Vance.'

'But we shan't be——' Jane began, then seeing Anthea's lifted eyebrow stopped. 'Oh, I—I don't know where Vance will want to live.' Wherever it is, she thought, I shan't be with him. Once she had thought *she* would live in Rome. With Gino. She frowned over the name Gino. He seemed like someone she had met in another life—it all seemed so far away.

It rained heavily all day, it was impossible to go out. Jane and Anthea played 'Happy Families' with Judy, and Jane read to her while Anthea disappeared to write letters. She came down again at teatime and paced about with her usual restlessness. After dinner she sat smoking and flicking through the pages of a magazine and then, abruptly, she stood up with a murmured excuse and went out of the room.

Jane went on trying to read her book, but her mind was not on it. She heard the wind rattling the shutters, the sough and the beat of the waves on the rocks below. She must have been sitting there some time before Anthea's light steps sounded on the stairs from the hall and she came down into the sitting-room. She looked radiant, her green eyes shining like emeralds, her pale skin glowing.

'Jane, I've a favour to ask of you. Would you think it terrible of me if I flew to Athens tomorrow? Just for a day or so. I wouldn't ask it of you—I mean, you could come too, but you wouldn't be awfully mobile with your poor old leg. And I thought—if I went now, you could be with Judy and I wouldn't have to worry about leaving her.'

'But of course,' Jane said. 'I'm only too happy to stay here with Judy. It's the least I can do in return for your kindness.'

Anthea was all smiles.

'Oh, super! You're such a sweetie, I felt sure you wouldn't mind. Thanks loads, Jane. I feel rather frightful leaving you marooned in this abysmal weather, but perhaps after I've gone it will clear up.' She turned away. 'I must go and throw a few things into a suitcase—I'm leaving on the early plane.'

'I suppose you'll come back with Julian,' said Jane. She felt slightly stunned by Anthea's whirlwind arrangements.

Anthea didn't appear to hear her—she was gone again, leaving Jane to stare blankly after her. Oh well, it was only natural that Anthea should wish to be with her husband; he had said she liked to visit Athens. *Athens*. The name conjured up a city of legend and antiquity. Jane thought somewhat wistfully that she would love to go there herself. Perhaps she would; perhaps she would go to Athens when she left the Villa. Meanwhile, she was pleased to stay and look after Judy now as a small return to Anthea and Julian for their hospitality to her.

When Anthea left next day it was still raining, but the wind had dropped and the weather was less wild.

'There, you see,' Anthea said smilingly as she brushed a light kiss on Jane's cheek. 'The sun's bound to come out again soon, so it won't be too dreary for you. Take care of yourself and Judy and rest your leg lots. 'Bye, Jane.' She reached down for Judy's eager hug. ' 'Bye, my poppet. Be a good baby. I'll bring you back a surprise.'

She was gone, sleek, animated and smiling; beautiful in a suit of shocking pink angora jersey, under a white trench coat, leaving Jane and Judy to wave after her as the car shot up the driveway.

The Villa seemed quiet and empty, darkened by the rain outside. Judy was tearful. 'When's Mummy coming back? And Daddy? I wish we could have gone too, Jane. Why couldn't we?'

'Well, darling, Daddy's very busy with his business arrangements. I don't suppose he would have much time to spend with you.'

'Are they with Auntie Kay? I always go to Auntie Kay's 'n play with Simon. He's my friend.'

139

'I expect you'll see him again soon. Shall we put our raincoats on and go and see how Chiron is? He probably feels awfully lonely. We could take him some cake and a carrot.'

Judy's face brightened. 'Yes, let's. Poor Chiron! He'll be in his little house out of the rain, won't he?'

'I hope so.'

It was wet outside, but not drenchingly so. The leaves of the olive trees blew tremblingly, shaking down the raindrops on to their heads. Chiron, sheltering in his open-ended hut, along with another donkey, greeted them with enthusiasm and stood munching stale cake with his furry ears laid back for Judy to rub, his brown eyes half closed with pleasure at their attentions. The other donkey was petted too and given a share of the delicacies Judy had brought with her.

After lunch and Judy's midday rest, a watery sun appeared briefly and the two of them walked down the winding steps to the beach to scramble about over the piles of driftwood. Judy was thrilled, retrieving strange objects; shells, stones, branches of wood, an old cauldron, a length of rubber tubing. Jane had difficulty in persuading her to leave any of it behind.

Jane spent a quiet evening reading; without Anthea's restless presence it was easier to settle to her book and although the big room felt strangely empty, the hiss and crackle of the log fire was a compensation.

In the morning it was raining again. A steady deluge that blotted out the tossing sea and the distant mountains. Jane began to realise how the lush and verdant green of Corfu had come about, when it rained it rained *thoroughly*, no two ways about that.

She gave Judy a reading lesson, pointing out words and objects in the big picture book and encouraging her to form letters on her miniature blackboard. Then it was lunch-time again and Judy's rest. Jane began to feel some of Anthea's unsettledness. She read and then put the book down. She

140

wrote another letter, mended a pair of tights, decided to wash her hair.

It was teatime and her hair was loose about her shoulders and almost dry when Judy jumped up, crying,

'I can hear the car. The car's come! Mummy's back—and Daddy!' She flew to the door, calling over her shoulder, 'Hurry, Jane—hurry! Mummy and Daddy have come back!'

More slowly, Jane rose to her feet, pushing back her long hair, smoothing down the tunic top of her pants suit. She followed Judy up the shallow steps into the hall, and as she did so, heard a car door slam and felt a sudden thrill of anticipation. If Julian had returned Vance would be with him. It was odd, but she knew she would be glad to see him again.

The front door opened and as Julian walked in, Judy hurled herself at him, screaming,

'Daddy—Daddy—Daddy!' and reached her eager arms round to hug his knees.

'Hello, my precious. *What* a welcome!' He picked her up and kissed her, then said over her shoulder, 'Hello, Jane.'

'Hello. How nice to see you back. Did you have a good flight?'

'Fair enough.' He put Judy down to the floor, and pushed a hand through his brown hair. 'Glad to be back, though. It's been non-stop. I'm flaked out, I don't mind telling you.' He walked towards the stairs. 'How have you been, Jane? And Anthea? Where is she?'

Jane stared at him.

'Anthea? But—but surely she's with you. She went away two—days ago.'

He swung round. '*Went away?* What on earth do you mean? Went away *where?*'

Jane stared at Julian, at his pale tired face, and untidy hair falling across his frowning forehead.

She said slowly, 'She flew to Athens on—on Wednesday. To—to be with you.'

CHAPTER ELEVEN

JULIAN backed slowly down the stairs and stopped to stare at her.

'I don't understand. Anthea didn't contact the Grande Bretagne where we were staying.' He frowned, running a thin hand through his untidy brown hair. 'She must have gone to stay with her friend Kay Alwyn. But why run off now, when we were due back here?'

Jane shook her head.

'I—I've no idea. The night before she left she told me she was going to telephone you and when she had done so she came in and said she was going to Athens. I naturally assumed it was to join you.'

'She didn't speak to me—and the hotel didn't give me any message. You must have got it wrong, Jane.' He paused and then his anxious face brightened. 'I think I know what happened. She tried to reach me by phone and when she couldn't she got through to Kay and arranged to go to her. And of course, by the time she reached Kay's and had tried to contact me again I was on my way back. Yes, that's it. I'm sure. I'll give Kay a ring this evening and expect I'll find Anthea is with her.' He turned to go up the stairs again, saying over his shoulder, 'Excuse me now, Jane. I'm going to shower and change and then perhaps we can have a drink together before dinner and catch up with our news.'

'Yes, all right, Julian. See you.'

Judy ran after him, catching hold of his hand.

'When is Mummy coming back? She's bringing me a present. Did you bring me something, Daddy?'

'Perhaps. We shall have to unpack my case and find out, won't we?'

Together they went up the stairs, Judy chattering happily, Julian's voice sounding happier and more relaxed as he answered her.

Jane went into the sitting-room where the log fire glowed a rosy welcome. She was puzzled. It seemed odd that Anthea hadn't left a message at the hotel where Julian was staying, even if she had been unable to contact him personally. Odder still to fly to Athens and not be with her husband, but stay at a friend's. But Julian had not seemed surprised at that possibility. Perhaps with a tight schedule of business meetings lined up for him Anthea had decided she might be in the way and that it would be more convenient for her to stay with her friend Kay.

After a drink and the appetising dinner Hestia had prepared for them Julian looked less tired. He stretched out in one of the low armchairs and said,

'It's good to be back here. Even in the rain. I'll go and telephone Kay in a few minutes, but at the moment I must say it's pleasantly restful by this fire. How have you been, Jane? I hope it's not been too dull for you on your own. Pity you couldn't have gone to Athens too—it's a fine city and the weather's better there than here at this time of year.'

'I should like to see the city, it sounds so fabulous—the Acropolis and the Agora, and what is that old part called—the old town?'

'The Plaka.'

'Yes, that's it. I hope to go and explore it all some time, but actually, at the moment, I wouldn't be able to walk very far and that would have spoilt things.'

'Yes. How is the leg? I hope it's better.'

'Lots better, thank you, just a bit stiff at times, especially after a lot of standing or walking.'

Julian yawned suddenly.

'Sorry, Jane. No reflection on your company, but I'm dead beat.' He rose slowly to his feet. 'If you'll excuse me I'll put that phone call through to Athens and then retire, I think.'

'Of course, you must be tired.'

143

After he had left the room she sat staring into the flickering flames, aware of a vague sense of depression, of disappointment. Disappointment over what? The fact that Vance hadn't returned with his brother? Absurd. She didn't care whether he was here or in Athens or in Timbuctoo.

Yet the evening felt flat, anticlimactic, and Jane couldn't understand why. She picked up her book again, determined not to sit brooding, and by concentrating hard upon the sense of the story she had read almost through a chapter when she heard Julian come down the steps leading from the hall into the sitting-room. She glanced up, the words 'Did you get through to Anthea?' on her lips, but one look at Julian's frowning troubled face as he flung himself into the recently vacated chair stayed her.

For a long moment he stared at the fire, biting his lip, rubbing a hand nervously over his mouth and chin, drumming on the arm of the chair with the other hand. At last he said with an almost explosive abruptness,

'I can't understand it. Anthea's not with the Alwyns. She's at the Grande Bretagne. I telephoned there after I'd spoken to Kay, in case there had been a message and the office told me Mrs. Morley had booked into the hotel but had gone out somewhere.' He paused, biting his lip. 'Vance is still there—he stayed on to tie up the ends of the deal, but he was out too. I asked to speak to him. He—he must be with Anthea.'

Jane wanted to say, 'What's wrong with that? Why shouldn't he be?' but something in Julian's brooding expression stopped her.

She said gently, 'Well, you know where she is, so you needn't worry any more. I expect she and—and Vance will be back in a few days.'

He didn't answer, only went on staring into space. Without turning his head to look at her he said, after a long silence,

'I suppose you don't know about Anthea and Vance. He

didn't tell you.'

She frowned in puzzlement. 'Tell me? Tell me what?'

Now Julian looked round at her, staring almost angrily as if, in some way, she was to blame.

'That they were engaged to one another. Oh, I can see that's come as a surprise. Now you know how *I* feel—wondering, suspicious. Jealous.'

Jane swallowed on the sense of shock Julian's words had engendered. Vance once engaged to Anthea? What an extraordinary facet to their relationship. Yet it explained so many things that had puzzled her—Vance's aloof manner to his sister-in-law, his seeming rudeness. Anthea's gentle acceptance of this, her sometimes beguiling sweetness as if she refused to be rebuffed.

Other things came back to her. The way Vance had said that the rift between himself and Julian had not been caused by business alone, but through a personal matter. The way he had once said that people couldn't change the way they felt about someone, even if they wanted to. He must have been—he must still be, in love with Anthea. And he had brought her, Jane, to Corfu in the role of his fiancée so that she would act as a buffer between himself and Anthea.

A slow anger began to burn through her. Yet what justification was there for that? She and Vance had struck a bargain. She was to pretend to be his fiancée and that would cancel out the debt she owed him for the hospital bill and the wrecked car.

'You see'—Julian went on—'it affects you too, doesn't it? You don't like it either.'

She wanted to say, 'I don't care. I'm not in love with Vance, as you are with Anthea,' and then she thought how mean and unworthy she and Julian were in their doubts. So Anthea was in Athens at the same time as Vance. At the same hotel. So what? It didn't necessarily mean they were conducting an affair, it was simply the result of a mix-up in arrangements, because Anthea had not contacted Julian in

145

time to find that he had left the hotel just when she was leaving the Villa Tyche.

She said carefully, choosing her words,

'It doesn't worry me, Julian. After all, even if Anthea *was* once engaged to Vance, the fact is, she fell in love with you and married you.' She added, for Julian's sake, 'And Vance is engaged to me and he is in—in love with me.'

Julian got up from his chair and walked across the room.

'Yes, of course. I'm sorry, Jane. I don't mean to worry or upset you. Of course Vance cares for you—that's obvious. It's just that——' He broke off, staring down at the floor. 'The fact is, Anthea—Anthea never has been in love with me. I was crazy about her, even when she was engaged to Vance. Then, when he quarrelled with Father and left the business, Anthea broke off her engagement to him. She said that he was acting stupidly—that they weren't suited. I think she hoped to bring Vance to his senses, but he cleared off just the same. For over a year no one heard from him— he never wrote, not even to Anthea. After a while Anthea turned to me and when I asked her to marry me, she said yes.'

'Then she must have loved you,' Jane said gently.

'In a way. But you know what they say—there's always one who kisses and one who is kissed. I'm the one who kisses. Anthea just—submits.'

Jane flung out a hand.

'Don't say things like that. And don't brood and worry and imagine things that aren't there. It's just a coincidence —a mix-up of plans, that Anthea and Vance are together in Athens—at the same hotel. It doesn't mean anything.' She said again, in reassurance, 'I'm not worried.'

Julian came over to her, an attempt at a smile on his thin face.

'Bless you, Jane. You're a great help. I suppose it's all in my mind—because I'm unsure of myself.' He shrugged. 'Perhaps too, because I've been ill and a drag on Anthea and I know she gets fed-up at times and bored with me. In a way, I've always been jealous of Vance—quite apart from the fact that he was once engaged to Anthea. He's such a positive character—he knows what he wants to do and does it. And makes a success of his life. I know Anthea admires him still—it was she who suggested that we should ask him to come and help me over this Italian merger. If it comes off, and it's practically in the bag, it will give the firm such a financial boost we shall never look back. If we'd missed it, things could have gone quite badly for us. I just wasn't up to coping—and no one else in the firm could have done the job, so I listened to Anthea and wrote to Vance. And he came. Quite honestly, I was worried stiff how things would turn out, but when he brought you along with him, everything seemed to fall into place, go right.'

'Thank you,' said Jane, seeing more clearly, with every word Julian spoke, the motive behind Vance's actions. What Julian didn't know, and never would know, was that her being at the Villa Tyche as Vance's fiancée was a complete fake. If he had known that, his fears of Vance, his suspicions might not so easily have been allayed. For a moment, like Julian a few minutes ago, she had a picture in her mind of Vance and Anthea together in Athens. Dining at some restaurant, dancing perhaps? Anthea so beautiful, so alluring. And Vance? Vance was still in love with her, if he hadn't been why would he have gone to such lengths as to bring an almost stranger to his brother's home pretending to be his fiancée? It could only be as a barricade behind which to hide. Because he was unable to trust his own feelings for Anthea.

She said slowly, 'When is Vance coming back?'

Julian shot her a quick, almost curious glance.

'Haven't you heard from him?'

'No, I—he's not much of a letter writer.'

'Really? He used to be. Perhaps it's a case of busman's holiday since writing's been his job.'

'Yes, perhaps.' Something in her voice, a flatness, an indifference caused him to look at her again.

'Cheer up. Vance is bound to be back within the next few days. Anthea too.'

'Yes.' She was glad he sounded more cheerful himself, more certain.

'I'll say goodnight, then. See you in the morning.'

'Yes. Goodnight, Julian.'

At the foot of the steps leading to the hall he half turned.

'Thanks for being such a comfort, Jane. I'm glad you're going to be one of the family.'

Feeling an absolute fraud, she managed to smile. 'Thank you.'

After he had gone, she lay back in the armchair staring into the dying fire. She knew now why she was here. Because Vance was still in love with Anthea. Of course it was no business of hers, she was not emotionally involved. Yet Jane was troubled in a way she found hard to analyse. It must be because she saw the inherent dangers of the situation she told herself, as at last she rose tiredly and made her way to bed.

Jane slept badly although the night outside was quiet and the storm seemed to have spent itself. She had queer confused dreams in which she kept encountering Vance, but every time she tried to speak to him he turned away or disappeared down endless corridors.

Surprisingly, she woke to fine weather. This morning the sky was soft and pearly, the sea a milky blue. Far away across the Straits the mountains of Albania glittered with the first capping of snow. The bay looked serenely beautiful, the olive trees surrounding it now more grey than green with the coming of autumn.

Julian was anxious to go through some papers he had brought back from Athens with him, so after breakfast he excused himself to Jane.

'Could I help in any way?' Jane asked. 'You know I did a lot of correspondence and figure work with Vance.'

'I know. And I'd be glad of your assistance in the ordinary way, but these are just things I want to check. I'm also going to try and contact Anthea, and see what's happening.'

Judy pouted, 'Oh, Daddy, I wanted you to come with me. I wanted to show you what a lot of things there are down on the beach. Jane and I brought lots up to the garden, didn't we, Jane? I want to show you those too.'

Julian smiled.

'Later, darling. I'll come and find you and we'll go and look at that treasure trove of yours.'

Judy repeated the word with a frown of concentration.

'Treasure trove. That's nice. Treasure trove.' She swung round. 'Jane, let's go and see my treasure trove.'

Jane smiled, catching hold of the small hand held out to hers.

'Why not? Shall we go down to the beach first?'

'Yes. Yes, let's!'

The flowers growing on either side of the steps were lifting their heads after the battering of rain. Geraniums were aromatic in the morning sunshine, a few blue-mauve Morning Glories straggled through wet leaves, bougainvillea, browned from the wind and rain, still produced crimson and purple flowers. Jane, limping down the steps, followed more slowly after Judy's small flying figure.

When she reached the beach Judy was already darting about among the scattered sea-wrack. When she saw Jane she waved and held something up in her hand.

'Look, Jane! Look at this. Isn't it super? It's a *picture*!' She came running back to Jane brandishing what seemed like a square of wood.

Jane took it from her and stared down at the blurred outline of figures in faded colours painted on the piece of wood. It looked like part of a mural, perhaps part of some ship's decoration.

'Isn't it super?' Judy said again. 'It's a picture for my bedroom.'

'Well,' Jane began doubtfully, 'it's rather worn—it must have been in the sea a long time.'

149

Judy seized it and clutched it tightly in both hands.

'I *like* it. Look, that's a lady's face—and a bit of tree. Let's take it to Daddy and ask him to clean it for me.'

'Daddy's busy at the moment. I'll help you clean it. But shall we see first if there's anything else exciting?'

Judy hesitated, then laid the broken treasure carefully down on a piece of rock.

'All right. I'll put it there. Let's walk this way—there's lots more things up here.'

No other spoils of any significance having been discovered, Judy retrieved her cherished 'picture' and together they climbed slowly up the steps to the top terrace. The sun was hot, the sea shimmered below them; it was a perfect day, as those other earlier days had been.

'I'm going to show this to Daddy,' Judy called over her shoulder, and before Jane could stop her, she was gone, racing into the Villa, clutching her booty in her arms. Jane hesitated, then, her leg aching somewhat after the steep climb from the beach, she subsided into one of the cane chairs to rest before going in to wash and tidy before lunch.

A step sounded on the terrace behind her and expecting to see Julian, she turned her head, but it was Hestia.

'Excuse, please, but is someones asking for you, Mademoiselle Jane!'

Jane sat up.

'Asking for *me*? Who is it, Hestia?'

'Is gentlemans——' Hestia began, then stopped, looking back to the sliding door of the sitting-room. Jane, glancing in the same direction, saw the figure of a man walk through and on to the terrace. For a moment he paused, staring towards her and then he came forward again.

She was already standing up, staring in incredulous fashion, as if she couldn't believe her own eyes. She heard Hestia murmur a 'Please excuse', before the girl hurried away out of sight. She watched the man coming nearer, unable still to speak or smile or give a greeting. And then he spoke, saying, with a flash of white teeth in the smooth brown of his face, '*Jane!* Jane, *cara mia*, so it is really you. So at last I have found you!' and the next moment she was in Gino's arms.

CHAPTER TWELVE

IT was like something in a dream. It couldn't really be happening, that Gino was here, kissing her, murmuring endearments at once familiar yet unreal. Jane was startled, almost shocked. It was as if a stranger were kissing her. She managed, with difficulty, to free herself and say, almost stammeringly,

'Gino, I can't—how did you—what are you doing *here*?'

He smiled, the warm caressing smile she had almost forgotten. 'You are surprised? You cannot believe that it is I?' He shook his head, his handsome curly brown head. Had he always been so incredibly good-looking? Jane thought, still dazed at the sight of him yet responding to the charm, the warm animal magnetism that had first enthralled her.

'I could not believe that you would be here—I thought surely it will be all a—what you call—wild duck chase?'

'Goose chase,' Jane interposed.

He was still holding her, but lightly, one hand on either of her arms. Now he gave her a slight shake and said,

'Goose, duck, swan, it is no matter. I have found you and now you must tell me what you are doing here. Is it with friends you stay, or do you have work? And why did you run away from me and come to this place?'

'How did you find *me*?' Jane countered slowly.

'At first it was difficult. I enquire of many people, many places. The office where you had worked, but it was closed and no one nearby could tell me. At your apartment it was the same—the old *signora*—the *portiera*—she knew nothing. Only that you had left luggage. My friend Enrico Baldoni, he too knows nothing, only that you have written saying you cannot work for him. I am despairing, but I do not give up hope that I shall find my Jane again.' He gazed down at her, his eyes bright and ardent. 'Did you think I should so easily let you go?'

Jane's head seemed to be spinning. She said dazedly,

'I—I thought you would forget about me. You had—you were engaged to Francesca.'

He shook his head.

'No more. *Finito*. We have talked together—we find out things alike. Francesca has met a friend in South America —he plans to visit her in Rome. I tell her I too love someone else and so together we are brave. We tell our parents— our family. We say it is not right that we should be affianced, and in the end all is understood.' He lifted his arms in mid-air. 'We are free—free as birds.' His hands fell to his sides and he caught hold of both her hands. 'Is it not *meraviglioso?*—wonderful, *cara mia?*'

Jane didn't know what to say. She was overwhelmed by the turn of events and too stunned to adjust to the fact that Gino was seemingly still in love with her and was now free of his engagement to his cousin. Once she would have thrown herself into his arms and echoed his words. Cried, 'Yes, yes, it is *meraviglioso*. I'm so happy. I love you, Gino.'

Now no such words would come. She stood, zombie-like, within the circle of his embrace and could think of nothing to say except, 'How *did* you find me?'

He smiled proudly.

'It was the *portiera*. I had not given up—I told myself that if you had left luggage she might hear from you and so I call often and ask her, "What news of the Signorina Roper?" and then one day she tells me she has letter from you. Can you imagine how I feel? I am overjoyed but puzzled. Why are you in Corfu? It is not summer—holidays are over. I guess you have work you do, and I make plans to visit the island. The ferry from Brindisi, it no longer sails, but I have a friend and he has a boat—he does not mind that the weather is not good. All the same, we wait for the storms to pass and then we come. We are here.' His handsome face darkened reproachfully. 'Why do you

153

not say you are glad to see me?'

'Oh, I am. Very glad. It's super to see you again. It's just that——' Jane's voice trailed away inadequately.

He said quickly, 'Do you worry that I shall be an embarrassment to you. I understand—it is that your employer may not wish me to be here with you. But we can meet—I am staying on the yacht with Roberto.'

'I'm not—not working here. I—I'm with friends.'

'Then it is simple. You will introduce me to these friends and I will say to them "I am in love with Jane." Surely then they will welcome me here.'

The complications were piling up with every moment that passed. How to tell Gino about Vance, how to explain the situation? Jane bit her lip, hesitatingly, and Gino, with a sudden movement, pulled her into his arms and said, 'There has been enough talk,' and bent his head to kiss her.

As he did so there was a sound on the terrace behind them and out of the corner of her eye Jane saw Julian coming towards them. Desperately she struggled free of Gino and gasped, smoothing her hair and making an attempt at composure.

'Here is—this is—please, Gino.'

He let her go at the moment Julian caught sight of them, and Jane could only hope he had seen nothing more untoward than herself standing in rather too close proximity to a strange young man.

Julian halted. 'Oh, hello, Jane. I came to look for you.'

'Did you? This is—I'd like to introduce a friend of mine. Gino Abetti. He—he's called quite unexpectedly. Gino, this is Julian Morley.'

Gino put his hand out.

'I am happy to meet you—to meet any friend of Jane's.'

Julian shook his hand, looking slightly puzzled.

'How d'you do.'

Gino gave an inclination of his head.

'I am well, thank you. And most happy to be here. To be

with Jane again.'

'Oh, that's fine. Are you on holiday in Corfu?'

'No. I have come to find Jane'—Gino looked fondly at Jane and reached for her hand. 'Even perhaps to take Jane back with me to Rome.'

Julian's look of puzzlement was now blank surprise.

'Back to Rome? How is that?' He glanced at Jane. 'No problems have come up, have they, Jane?'

'N-not really,' Jane answered untruthfully. She was nervous of what Gino, or for that matter, Julian was likely to say next.

Julian frowned. 'I came to tell you that I got through to the hotel in Athens and was informed that both Anthea and Vance had checked out. They left no message as to where they had gone.'

Jane stared. 'But they must be on their way back here, surely?'

Julian shrugged, his expression tight and unhappy.

'I suppose so. I—I'm in a fog about the whole thing. Why didn't Anthea contact *me* at the hotel, only go there after I'd left?'

He became aware of Gino's presence and added, 'Please excuse me speaking of—family matters. There has been a slight mix-up of arrangements.'

Gino inclined his head politely.

'Please, it is I who am in the way.' He frowned. 'We have not met before, Mr. Morley? Your name, it is familiar to me.'

'You've probably met my brother, Vance. He's in Athens at the moment.'

'*Vance*. That is not a common name.' The golden-brown eyes narrowed to regard Jane. 'I have heard of your brother —I think I have met him. Is this so, Jane?'

'I—I believe you—saw him in Rome.'

Gino's glance went back to Julian. He nodded darkly.

'Yes, I have seen him. He is like you, no? Yet not so like.' His hand sketched a shape. 'A bigger man, I think?'

155

'Yes, Vance is taller. Well, that's a coincidence, your being here and having met or seen Vance before. Will you stay and have lunch with us?'

'Thank you, you are most kind. I should like to do that.'

'Good. I'll tell them in the kitchen there'll be one extra.'

When he had gone Gino turned on Jane.

'What is this?' he demanded fiercely. 'What are you doing here with this man who—who accosted you in the Piazza Navona? Ah yes, I remember it all now—you pretended you were angry with him. Now I find you are friends—you stay with this man's family.'

'Gino, please,' Jane protested. 'Don't be so high-handed. You've dropped in here, out of the blue, and now start trying to take me over. I'm very happy to see you, but we—we can't start again where we left off. Everything's different. All—all sorts of things have happened since we said goodbye in Rome.'

Gino seized her hand. 'What things? What do you mean? Why do you torture me so?'

She had forgotten how intense, how dramatic he could be. She dreaded to think what scene would be perpetrated when he learned that she was engaged to Vance. Gino would never understand how it could all have happened so quickly. She wished she could explain the situation to him, but without seeing Vance first she felt she must not do so. Gino might say something to reveal the masquerade to Julian or Anthea.

She said unhappily,

'I—I—don't feel the same towards you as—as I did. Everything's changed.'

He struck his chest with one hand.

'I have not changed. I am true to you, Jane. I love you. Do you not understand? I am free of that family *imbroglio* —free to ask you to be my wife. I honour you, I respect you. You are someone with much character as well as being a lovely person—beautiful and adorable. I discover that in Rome when you say to me, "Goodbye, Gino. I am not to be

156

treated lightly." '

'Oh, Gino!' She said the words on a sigh—of sympathy for Gino, of regret for what might have been. 'Please don't say such things. You make me feel so—so sorry.'

He caught both her hands in his.

'For why are you sorry? You loved me in Rome—why should you not love me now? It is only a few weeks since we were together—your heart cannot have changed in this little time, Jane. Jane, *cara mia*.'

He spoke like a book, the words flowed from him, ardently, harmoniously, a little unreal.

She bit her lip, 'I have changed,' wanting to put the entire encounter on an honest basis. But in a few moments they would be sitting down to lunch. If only they could get through the meal without Julian disclosing the fact that she was Vance's fiancée all would be well. Afterwards she would tell Gino she was engaged and say goodbye to him, and there would be no scenes, no dramas enacted in public. Looking at him now, handsome, warmly attractive, she asked herself how it was she could think coolly and dispassionately of saying goodbye to him. Once the thought that he would have broken free of an earlier commitment and come to find her like this and ask her to be his wife would have been happiness beyond belief. It wasn't as if she was *really* engaged to Vance; that they were *really* in love with one another and going to be married. That was just an act put on for the benefit of Julian, of Anthea too, perhaps, so she would not guess that Vance was still in love with her.

She said with a sudden tiredness,

'It must be nearly time for lunch, Gino. Don't let's talk any more about this, but after—afterwards, I'll explain.'

'Explain? Explain what?' He came after her as she turned away to the sitting-room entrance.

'I'll tell you later. Now I'm going to wash my hands and tidy. Will you sit here and wait—Julian will be back any moment.'

157

She went upstairs, glad for a moment to have escaped the problem of Gino. Then as soon as she was in her room Jane imagined Julian returning to the sitting-room to find Gino there and perhaps speaking of herself and Vance, and she instantly wanted to dash downstairs again.

Brushing out her long hair, she found the thought of Vance superseding that of Gino in her mind. She knew Julian was worrying over Anthea's mysterious departure to Athens and her meeting with Vance, that he feared the meeting had been prearranged. Jane felt sure this wasn't so. Surely Vance would never have gone to the length of bringing a pretend fiancée to his brother's home, as a sort of shield between himself and the girl he had been formerly engaged to, unless he was anxious to remain aloof from Anthea?

But what of Anthea? Anthea, who on Julian's admission had never been in love with her husband. Was she still hankering after Vance? Looking back on small incidents it seemed to Jane that Anthea was still attracted to him.

She felt tired and full of confusion, and she wished fervently that Gino had never put in an appearance. How could this be? Only a few weeks ago she had been overwhelmingly in love with him, had longed for him to be free and to love her in return. Now, after a brief absence, he no longer had the power to make any impact upon her. Jane asked herself again and shied away from the answer, hidden somewhere deep down inside.

When she returned to the sitting-room it was to find Gino smiling and seemingly content, drinking a Campari soda and talking to Julian. So far, so good. No jarring revelation had been made. She accepted a Martini and sat down some little way from Gino. Judy came in and perched on the arm of Jane's chair and gazed admiringly at their guest.

Despite Gino's voluble charm, lunch was an uneasy meal. Conversation seemed an effort to Julian, who every now and then fell into an introspective silence, and Jane herself was on tenterhooks in case some reference was made to her presence in the household. But Judy's happy chatter helped to fill the awkward gaps and Gino, who had the Italian's affectionate response to children, smiled and talked to her, and somehow, at last, the meal was over.

Julian rose abruptly from the table.

'If you'll excuse me, I won't take coffee with you. I—I have some things to attend to.' He gave Jane a strained smile. 'I'll leave you to entertain your guest. Come along, Judy. Time you went upstairs with Hestia.'

Judy pouted but allowed herself to be led away. Gino, turning with Jane towards the terrace, watched her go, saying with a smile,

'She is *deliziosa*, that one.' Then his expression changed. He said more soberly, 'Now, please, you are to explain to me what has happened. How is it that you have come here, Jane?'

She looked away from him, staring at the milky sea, the distant mountains, silver-tipped in the sunshine.

'I came away from Rome because—because you were engaged to Francesca. I saw the—the problems that could arise between us and I thought the best thing to do was to leave the city. I planned to go to Naples, to stay with a girl-friend there. And then—then I met Vance Morley again and he—offered me a lift in his car as far as there.' She broke off and after a short pause Gino's voice said from close behind her, 'So?'

It was difficult to explain without revealing her strange situation with Vance. And she couldn't confide this to Gino, it was Vance's business. She said slowly,

'I—had an accident driving his car on the road near Cassino and was in hospital with a broken arm and concussion. Vance was—very kind. He stayed near by and—and saw to things. My arm was in plaster—I couldn't do anything much, and he offered me a sort of job here.'

Gino frowned.

'I am sorry, Jane. I see that you are limping when I arrive—you have had a bad time? If only I had known!'

159

'Thank you, but it's all right now. I opened up the old wound while swimming, but it's healed again.'

'This job—you said you were not working? That these people are your friends.'

'They are, in a way. They—Julian Morley and his wife —Vance too—have been most kind to me. I haven't a job in the real sense of the word—I mean, I'm not a paid employee. But it so happens that Julian and Vance are negotiating a merger between their family business and an Italian firm in Milan. I've been able to do typing and so on for them.'

Gino was still frowning.

'I cannot understand how this—this Vance whom you met only once, twice, in Rome should play so important a part in your affairs.' He stared at her. 'He is in love with you, yes?'

'Of course not. It—it's just circumstances that have thrown us together.'

'But you tell me you are changed. It must be that this is some other man who comes into your life. How otherwise should you alter in so short a time?'

How indeed, Jane thought. But that's the way it is. I'm not in love with Gino any more. I thought I was, but now I see him again I know I'm not. But how it's happened I can't explain.

She said slowly, choosing her words with care,

'I—don't feel the same as I did, Gino. I know that. Oh, please, don't look like that,' for his face was a mirror, the gaiety and warmth dimming instantly to despair, the golden eyes shadowing. 'I—I hate to say it. It's wonderful of you to have come all this way to find me and I wish with all my heart that everything could be the same as it was. But it isn't, and it can't be.'

He caught his full lower lip between his teeth.

'I will not believe that, Jane. We have been parted—you feel strange with me. But if I stay, if we are together I will make you love me again.'

160

She hated hurting him. Despite his veneer of sophistication there was something childlike, vulnerable about Gino. She said with difficulty, 'It won't be like that. I know it won't.'

How could she know, how could she be so certain? Little more than a month ago she had been wildly in love with him, now he seemed no more than a handsome boy whom she liked, but that was all.

He gazed at her, his eyes melancholy and full of pleading.

'Don't send me away, *cara mia*. I have come these miles to see you again—am I not allowed the chance to be with you for a little while. Perhaps to try to change your mind for you?'

What could she say to that except hesitantly, reluctantly,

'Of course, Gino, if that's what you want. You know that I'm pleased to see you again—as—as a friend. It's just that—anything else would be a waste of time.'

He smiled, his eyes glowing with light, and reached out to catch her hands in his.

'No time is wasted with you, Jane. I am here and you are here and we will talk and be happy with one another.' He swung round, gesturing towards the sea and the mountains and the olive groves. 'This is a beautiful place—such views. I have a car—a hired one—we can drive somewhere. I will take you to Roberto's yacht and we will dine with him on the *Minerva*. It will be like old times, I think. Will you come tonight?'

Jane hesitated, feeling that events were rushing away with her, seeing in Gino's mercurial expansiveness more complications.

'Perhaps not tonight. It might be difficult to get away.'

'Then tomorrow. Tomorrow I will come and fetch you— we will go to Corfu or to the so beautiful Paleocastritsa. And at night you will have dinner with Roberto and me. You may bring your friend Mr. Morley, if you wish. I will return his kind hospitality to me in that fashion. Say yes, Jane. Promise to come.'

161

She said half in laughter, half in despair, 'Oh, Gino!'

'That means "yes", I think? Now, shall we sit down over there and drink some of the coffee that was brought to us, unless it has become cold.'

They sat down on the terrace and Jane poured the coffee and they drank it. Gino smoked a thin cheroot and was his old self, as gay and charming as ever. He recounted amusing stories of his life in Rome, described Francesca's young admirer, told her of the new car he hoped to buy, of the expansion of business interests, and soon Jane was relaxed in his company and laughing at his jokes, and was amazed to find, when Julian put in an appearance, that it was after four o'clock.

Gino scrambled to his feet and apologised for staying so long. He would not sit down again, but extended the invitation to Julian to dine on the yacht the next evening and then insisted that he must leave.

Jane walked out to the courtyard with him, to where an unfamiliar grey car was parked.

'It has been wonderful to be with you, *cara mia*. Tomorrow I will come and we will drive for lunch somewhere. Shall we say around eleven o'clock?'

She was being carried along at breakneck speed towards some end she couldn't visualise.

'I—yes, all right, about eleven.'

He would have caught her to him, but she put a hand against his chest and said firmly,

'Goodbye, Gino.'

He shrugged and slid into the driving seat.

'*Arrivederci*, my Jane. Until tomorrow.'

The car started up and moved away towards the gateway. Over his shoulder Gino called out something and as he drove out on to the road Jane walked slowly after him saying,

'What? What did you say?'

He pulled the car round and braked, putting his head through the window to smile and say,

'I say thank you, Jane. You have made me so happy. *Beato.*'

She waved a dismissing hand and at the same moment saw that a car coming along the opposite side of the road was now slowing down, as if to turn in at the gates of the Villa. Jane stared. It looked like a taxi. There were two people in the back of it.

Gino, ignoring the car, reached through his open window and caught hold of her two hands in his and pressed an ardent kiss in the palm of each, before saying huskily,

'Tomorrow, Jane.'

Jane scarcely heard him. She pulled her hands back as if they were on fire, aware only that, as Gino drove away, the man staring through the back window of the taxi as it passed through the gateway of the Villa Tyche was Vance.

CHAPTER THIRTEEN

SLOWLY, reluctantly she walked forward. Vance was already helping Anthea out of the taxi and as he did so, Julian appeared in the doorway of the Villa. At the sight of Anthea the frowning strain of his expression faded and his face lit up in a relief of happiness.

'Anthea darling, I'd no idea you were on your way home. Wonderful to have you back again!' and reaching out his arms he bent his head to kiss her.

Anthea moved slightly so that her cheek was pressed against his.

'Lovely to be home.' Her voice was cool. Gently, firmly, she detached herself. 'Really, darling, anyone would think I'd been gone a month!'

Julian kept his arm about her shoulders, smiling fondly down at her.

'It seems like a month.'

Jane had come to a halt beside Vance and now she forced herself to look up into his frowning dark face. She said hesitantly, 'Hello.'

His eyes were narrowed, they glittered like chips of granite through half-closed lids.

'Hello, Jane.' He added sardonically, '*Darling*,' and caught hold of her. The next second she was in his arms and he was kissing her, his mouth harsh and brutal on her own. When she gasped for breath, and struggled to protest, he moved his lips to mutter fiercely against her cheek, 'You didn't waste much time.'

'Wh-what do you mean?'

'Wasn't that your Italian friend I saw leaving just now?' Abruptly he released her and in an altered tone said suavely, 'You look better. How's the leg been?'

Aware of Julian's smiling gaze, of Anthea's watchful

look, Jane swallowed down the spate of fury that had surged through her, the crazy impulse to hit out at Vance as if in anger and resentment she would wipe away the sarcastic expression on his dark face.

'It—it's better, thank you.'

'Good.'

'Where did you two get to?' Julian broke in to say. 'I telephoned the Grande Bretagne several times and couldn't make contact with either of you.' He looked down at Anthea. 'I rang Kay—I thought you'd be with her.'

Anthea shrugged.

'Oh, Kay was tied up with a dozen things. It just wasn't convenient to stay. Of course I thought *you'd* be at the hotel, darling. It was such a surprise to find only Vance there.' She glanced round. 'Where's Judy? Do let's go in and find her.'

'Yes, all right, sweetheart.' He looked over his shoulder at Vance. 'Come and have a drink.'

'In a minute. I'll get the cases.' Vance watched his brother go into the Villa and then he turned to Jane and said,

'You've a little explaining to do.'

'Explaining? What about?' She was deliberately obtuse.

He said explosively,

'For God's sake, you know what about. That baby-faced boy-friend of yours. When did you send for him?'

'I didn't send for him. He—he just came. This morning.'

He gave a sound that could have been a laugh.

'He just *came*. Like that? I thought you said you hadn't written to him, hadn't sent him any address.'

'I hadn't. He—got it from the—the *portinaria*. I'd written to her with a forwarding address for letters.'

The cold grey gaze never left her face.

'I see. I suppose you hoped he would do just that—call and enquire. You're still hooked on him?'

Jane said furiously,

'What business is it of yours how I feel about Gino?

165

You're not *really* my fiancé, you know. If I still happen to be in love with him it's got nothing to do with you. And if he—he chooses to come all the way here to find me you can't possibly object.'

The formidable black eyebrows came down over the slitted eyes.

'But I do object, wholeheartedly. Oh, not on emotional ground, my dear. You can moon around for ever with your fascinating young friend as far as I'm concerned.' His deep voice hardened. 'Except for one thing. We made a bargain. You were to pretend while you were here to be my fiancée, and I don't want some amorous Lothario turning up on Corfu to spoil the effect.'

Jane had never felt so angry in her life. She had heard of people seeing red with rage, and that was just how she felt now—as if she saw Vance through a crimson cloud of temper. She heard her own voice saying with a vindictiveness she would have thought impossible,

'Oh, of course, I forgot. The effect—that must be preserved at all costs. The pretence—the façade. If—if people found out that after all I *wasn't* your fiancée they might discover the truth. That I'm only here as a blind, to hide the fact that you're in love with Anthea—in love with your brother's wife!'

His face was a mask. He said through gritted teeth,

'Where did you dream up that idea?'

She said more soberly,

'Julian told me you—you were once engaged to her. The idea seems to—worry him.'

'I don't see why it should—after all, Anthea chose to marry *him*, not me.' Vance's voice held a note of bitterness which caused Jane to turn her head to look at him.

'Julian thinks she married him on the rebound. After you left the family business and went away.'

'Julian seems to have told you a hell of a lot.' His mouth thinned to a set line. 'It's true Anthea was engaged to me, true that we quarrelled over my leaving the firm—she

166

wanted me to stay with my father because she thought there was no future in journalism. As for the rest'—he shrugged —'it's all water under the bridge now!'

There was a silence and then Jane said slowly,

'You are still in love with her, aren't you? That's the reason you brought me here, to act as a sort of buffer between you.'

He said curtly,

'If I am, it's no business of yours, as you told me about you and Gino, just now. Let's skip the personalities and stick to business. I can't have your—*friend* here—it's too tricky. You'll have to send him away. What you do after you leave the Villa will no longer be my concern, but while you are here, the situation between us must appear to be beyond question. Those are the terms we agreed upon.'

She sighed with a curious heaviness, the temper draining from her. It was true, then. Vance was still in love with Anthea. Had they arranged to meet in Athens after Julian had left? No, she couldn't believe that of him. He would never have gone to the lengths of bringing her, Jane, to Corfu with him if he had intended to do anything like that. He would surely not betray his brother.

She said on a sudden afterthought,

'Gino is coming here tomorrow—to take me out.'

He scowled—there was no other word for it.

'That's going to take a little explaining—with your dear fiancé just returned from afar. You'd hardly go off and leave him so soon, would you?' He broke off and then said sharply,

'What have you told Gino?'

'Nothing.' She bit her lip. 'I couldn't tell him we—we were engaged.'

'Because of shattering your own romance, I suppose. How the devil did you think you were going to dodge the issue? But it's just like a woman to prevaricate—to try the doublecross.'

'And talking of doublecrosses, what's happened to the

167

fiancée, the Italian girl Gino was tied up with?'

'It's all finished. He's free. Please don't talk about my doublecrossing anybody. I simply didn't tell Gino I was engaged to you because I didn't want to reveal *your* mixed-up affair—your involvement with Anthea.'

He ignored the jibe.

'I'm not sure what we should do.' He frowned consideringly. 'Perhaps the best thing is for you to see Gino and tell him you're sorry, you can't invite him here. Make some excuse—say we're ill, busy, anything. I shall be finished here in a couple of weeks—tell him to go back to Rome, that you'll see him there.' The grey eyes narrowed. 'If that's what you want.'

What did she want? Not to go to Rome, not to be with Gino. That was for certain. To stay here—near Vance? Was that what she wanted? And suddenly, despairingly, Jane knew that the only thing she wished, desired, longed for, was to never leave Vance.

It struck her with the impact of a thunderbolt and for a moment she couldn't speak. She had fallen in love with Vance. She knew it now; knew why she had been jealous of Anthea. Why, too, this time on Corfu had been like a golden dream. And why Gino's coming to find her had made little or no impression upon her.

He broke the long silence to say impatiently, 'Well?'

She swallowed on the dryness of her throat and said with admirable calmness,

'I—I'll try and see Gino. He's staying on a friend's yacht.' She struggled to remember the name and it came to her at last. 'It's called the *Minerva*.'

'I'll run you down to the old harbour first thing in the morning. What time did he arrange to be here?'

'About eleven.'

'Right. We'll go straight after breakfast.' He turned. 'Better go in and find the others. I'll bring Anthea's case.'

Jane walked away and into the villa. She couldn't bear the thought of seeing Anthea and she went slowly up the

168

stairs to her room, instead of going into the sitting-room. She sat down on the edge of the bed and stared at the wall facing her. Whatever happened she must never let Vance know how she felt about him. It was queer, really. Through all their arguments and quarrels she had felt the pull of his magnetism. She had resented it, tried to resist it, but still there had been times when she had succumbed to it. When he had kissed her on the terrace and she had responded to him, in spite of herself; and when he had said goodbye before leaving for Athens and she had wished then that he had kissed her again.

Two more weeks, he had said. Then the masquerade of being his fiancée would be over and they would say goodbye, two polite strangers who would never meet again.

I can't bear it, Jane thought, and pushed a fist against her midriff as if to push away the heavy ache that seemed to have settled there.

She stayed upstairs a long time, unable to brace herself to go down and put in a normal appearance. When finally she did go, she felt stiff with self-consciousness and went and sat down as far away from Vance as possible and concentrated all her attention on Judy.

Today, however, Judy was too excited by her mother's return to spare much time for Jane and she would have gone on dancing and chattering around Anthea if the latter, who had been sitting in one of the big armchairs staring moodily into her glass, had not looked up suddenly and said with a frown,

'Poppet, do stop jumping about like a jack-in-a-box, it gives me a headache. I'm tired—we had a rotten flight, nothing but delays.'

Judy's rosebud mouth fell open, her eyes were suddenly glassy with tears. She subsided into a heap at Anthea's feet, staring dumbly up at her mother. Julian put a hand on Judy's shoulder and said,

'Judy feels as I do—so pleased you're back with us that she doesn't know what to do.' He removed his hand and

169

clasped Anthea's, 'I was beginning to worry about you.'

'I can't think why. I've only been gone three days.'

'It was not knowing where you were.' Julian leaned forward to say earnestly, 'You shouldn't have gone away like that without leaving some message.'

'Oh, honestly!' Anthea's slim shoulders jerked, and in one graceful movement she was on her feet. 'I'm going upstairs to change.'

Julian stood up after her.

'I'll come with you.'

Anthea turned.

'Julian, *please*. I told you—I have a headache. I'm going to lie down for half an hour.'

'Darling, I'm so sorry——' but Anthea was already half-way across the room.

Vance, who had been sitting near the window glancing through some letters, lifted his head to say,

'There are some things here I'd like to go over with you, Julian, if you're not too tired. Could we go in the study?'

Julian, who had been staring blankly after Anthea, turned, frowningly.

'What did you say?' and when Vance repeated his remark, nodded to say, 'Yes, yes, of course.'

'Excuse us, won't you?' Vance said to Jane in passing her chair, and like Julian, she nodded and said,

'Yes, of course,' and found herself left alone in the big room.

The evening passed quietly and without incident except for one awkward moment when Julian remarked, as if for something to say,

'We had a visitor this morning, at least Jane did. Someone from Italy called to see her quite unexpectedly. Apparently he and a friend came to Corfu on the friend's yacht—a late holiday, I suppose.'

Anthea turned her head to look at Jane, one delicate eyebrow lifted in query.

'*He?*' There was a wealth of meaning in her voice.

170

Jane felt her cheeks colour under Anthea's gaze. She glanced quickly at Vance and then said,

'Yes, I—he's someone I knew when I was working in Rome.'

'How intriguing. Was *he* a courier too?'

'No, just—just someone I met there.'

Anthea's voice was thoughtful. 'He must be quite a *close* friend to have known your whereabouts and made the effort to call and see you. Do *you* know him, Vance? I hope you approve of his friendship with your fiancée?'

'I know him,' Vance said aloofly. 'Naturally Jane has friends of her own—as I do. We don't have to vet each other's acquaintances.'

'He sounds rather more than an acquaintance. Is he coming here again—I shall look forward to meeting him.'

'He's very good-looking,' Julian interposed. 'Judy fell for him—and I must say he was charming with her. Obviously fond of children.'

'The ultimate accolade—fond of children and animals,' Anthea observed mockingly. 'And handsome into the bargain. Really, Vance, I should be jealous if I were you.'

'I'm afraid he—he won't be able to call again,' Jane broke in. 'He has—they're probably leaving quite soon.'

'Yes——' Vance agreed. 'I'm taking Jane along in the morning to say goodbye to him.'

Anthea sighed. 'What a shame! I should have loved to have met him.'

That had been a narrow escape, Jane thought. There was something sharp, almost vindictive under Anthea's teasing manner. She had been in an odd mood since her return from Athens, offhand and impatient with Julian, almost ignoring Vance, except in this last small scene.

She had left for Athens in such a happy frame of mind and returned short-tempered and sharp-tongued. Whatever it was that had occurred in Athens had obviously upset her.

Anthea did not come to breakfast next morning and

Julian was not up either, so Jane and Vance took their rolls and coffee on the terrace together. Vance was more silent than usual, Jane tired and depressed after a restless night.

When the meal was over he glanced across to her and said,

'Shall we go? It may take a little time to find the actual boat.'

'Yes, I'm ready. I'll get a jersey.'

It was another fine morning, bright but cool. They were soon in the town, driving through the narrow streets past small shops filled with a profusion of fruit; beans, melons, grapes and green peppers, oranges, lemons, pomegranates and pears. She had never seen such lavishness. The Venetian style houses were flat-fronted, biscuit-coloured; between them ran narrow passageways and alleys, flights of steps, washing blowing in the morning breeze. They reached the sea front, the wide park with its clock tower and bandstand and the great grey Fortress high above the Old Harbour. Across the straits the mountains were blue against the sky, silver-tipped in the sun.

Vance parked the car near the harbour and led the way past the ferries and the large ships to where the yachts and smaller boats were moored.

'Wait here,' he said. 'I'll make some enquiries. The *Minerva*, you said?'

'Yes.' Jane stood leaning on the parapet, her long brown hair blowing round her shoulders. She was glad of the short-sleeved yellow jersey she had pulled over the white polo-necked sweater she was wearing, glad of the suede pants. She stared across the water, wondering how she was going to persuade Gino that it would be impossible for her to see him again. It wouldn't be easy, she was sure. But whatever had been between them was over, somehow she must convince him of that.

Vance was coming back to her, tall and lithe, his face brown above the navy polo sweater he wore, and her heart seemed to turn over at the sight of him. The sun shone on his blue-black head, and she thought, as she had thought before, that though he was not handsome, there was something outstandingly attractive about him.

'I've found out where the *Minerva* is moored. It's over that way. See the tall-masted ketch—and the big power boat alongside? It's past there.' He looked down at her from his great height, his face stern and set as it had been all morning. 'I'll go back to the car and wait for you.'

'All right.' She went on standing there, reluctant to face the scene she felt must lie ahead of her.

'I'm sorry to ask you to do this, but there's no alternative. You must see that. You're supposed to be engaged to me and I want to keep it that way. Until we leave Corfu, that is.'

How indifferently he said the words, how uncaring. She turned away to hide the unhappiness that engulfed her and hurried quickly along the quay in the direction Vance had indicated.

The *Minerva* was a small sleek yacht painted turquoise and white. A thickset man in a black jersey was polishing the rails and he looked up and smiled at Jane as she came alongside.

'*Buon giorno, signorina.*'

She answered him in Italian and his swarthy face creased in an even wider smile.

'May I speak to Signor Abetti, please?'

He lifted the rag in his hand into mid air.

'Signor Abetti, he is not here. Only Signor Marcesi. You wish to speak with him, no?'

She frowned in sudden dismay. Gino wasn't on the yacht. Did that mean—surely he had not left for the Villa Tyche so early?

'Thank you, Yes, I'd like to, if I may.'

In a matter of seconds a tall young man in a matelot shirt appeared in the hatchway. He bowed to Jane and said in excellent English,

173

'You are Signorina Rop-aire. How do you do? I have heard much—much of you from Gino. I am delighted to meet you,' and he bowed again over the hand he had taken in his, then added frowningly, 'But Gino, he has already left to keep his appointment with you. So happy, so eager is he to be with you he cannot wait, but tells me he will go at once. I think he has also to arrange about the car he wished to hire.'

'Oh!' was all Jane could answer. 'Oh dear, then I've missed him.'

Signor Marcesi looked puzzled.

'That is so. But would it not have been better for you to have awaited him at your villa? He told me you are a few kilometres out of Corfu.'

She bit her lip.

'Yes, it was silly of me to—to come like this. Only I was—was offered a lift into the town. I thought it would save Gino the trouble of coming all that way out.'

He shrugged.

'What a pity. Now you must return there. May I offer you coffee—something to drink before you leave?'

She shook her head.

'No, I—thank you so much, but I must go at once and find Gino. I'm so sorry to have troubled you. Goodbye, *signore*.'

He bowed over her hand yet again.

'It is no trouble. *Arrivederci, signorina.*'

She hurried down the narrow gangplank and along the quay and round the back of the building to where Vance had left the car. When she reached him she was breathless, but in a few hurried words she told Vance what had happened.

He frowned, stubbing out the cigarette he had been smoking. He said briefly, 'The devil!' and started up the car and moved forward almost before she had closed the door on herself.

'Perhaps we shall overtake him,' he said once as he drove with care but also with speed along the road which they had just come. 'Would you recognise the car? Keep an eye out for him.'

CHAPTER FOURTEEN

THERE was no sign of Gino anywhere between Corfu and the Villa Tyche, but when, at last, Vance turned into the gateway of the Villa Jane saw with apprehension the same grey car that Gino had driven away in the day before parked on the driveway.

She gave Vance a quick sideways glance and saw that he was frowning too.

'Prepare for some complications,' he said as he leaned over to push open the car door before sliding out himself. Jane followed more slowly after him, aware of a sense of trepidation as she went into the Villa.

The sitting-room was empty, but through the open window Jane glimpsed figures on the terrace, heard the sound of voices. She halted in her tracks until Vance's hand jerked her elbow as he said grimly, 'Come on. This is as much your doing as mine.'

Three heads turned at their approach, three faces stared at them in turn. Gino's handsome one, flushed and angry; Julian looking pale and strained, lined about the eyes as if he had not slept well, Anthea sat with curling mouth and green eyes narrowed to mocking derision.

She was the first to speak,

'Here come the happy couple. Or rather, the not-so-happy couple.' She gestured with a languid hand.

'Vance, I believe you've already met Signor Abetti and of course, Jane, you know him *very* well. At least, so he has just been telling us. I'm afraid he's been made most unhappy to hear of your'—she paused and added with delicate emphasis—'*engagement*. Apparently you didn't mention it to him yesterday.'

Gino was already on his feet, his golden eyes sullen on Jane's, his full lower lip set mutinously.

'How could you do this to me, Jane? Not to tell me—not to speak the truth of your association with Signor Morley, when I am here with you yesterday. You have humiliated me—and hurt me here—here,' and he struck his chest with his open hand.

Jane took a step towards him,

'I'm sorry, Gino, truly I'm sorry. I was going to tell you yesterday, but I—I thought—I hoped, that when I told you things were—were changed between us you would go away, and I wouldn't have to.'

'You have deceived me—you tell me in Rome you scarcely know this man—that it is only for a business arrangement you are here, and now I come and discover you are betrothed to him. What *is* truth and what is not in this affair?'

Vance spoke for the first time, saying in his deep drawling voice, 'It's my fault, not Jane's. Please don't blame her too much. It's true we didn't know one another very well in Rome, but later after Jane's accident we drew closer to one another. We—became engaged.' He paused, then added slowly, 'You must remember that at that time Jane thought *you* were engaged to someone.'

Gino gestured impatiently,

'That is over. I am in love with Jane. I come to find her and then'—his voice dropped a note—'she breaks my heart with her falseness. Telling me I may stay here and visit her. Today we make this plan to be together, and all the time she is engaged to you.' He turned on Jane. 'You lie to me. Yesterday when I am jealous of this man,' and he flung a hand out in Vance's direction, 'when I ask you if you are in love with him, what do you say to me? You say "No—no, I am *not* in love with him." That you are here to do typing. *Aah!*' And he made a fierce disparaging sound.

'I told you I—I wasn't in love with *you*, Gino. That everything was changed between us. Why couldn't you have gone away then?'

'Because you allow me to hope—is that not so? But now

if you tell me that everything is over I will go. I will never see you again.'

She bit her lip, aware that Julian had walked away out of earshot but that Anthea was still sitting on the hammock seat, staring down at her gently swinging foot, as if enjoying every moment of the drama.

Jane said quietly,

'Everything *is* over, Gino. I'm sorry. Sorry if I have hurt you or misled you. Will you forgive me and—and say goodbye as a friend?'

He turned his head to look at her, warm amber eyes misted with the tears that came so easily to him. He seemed unable to speak, but after a moment he said,

'I can never feel as a friend towards you, but goodbye, Jane.' He took her hand in his and held it before touching it briefly with his lips. He said something in a low voice that sounded like Latin. '*Tu mihi sola eras.*' Then he let go of her hand and glancing briefly at Vance and Anthea and lastly at Julian's turned back, he said '*Addio*' and walked quickly away.

Vance stared after him.

'Poor devil! I never liked him more.'

Jane said nothing. She was too full of the emotion of the moment, and to hide how she felt she walked across to the balustrade and stared at the shining sea. From behind her she heard Anthea say, 'What a theatrical young man! but I felt sorry for him. He was quite shattered when he arrived here this morning and learned from Julian that Jane was supposed to be engaged to you. I say supposed because I don't think we've got to the bottom of this mysterious affair yet. I thought there was something phoney about it from the moment you both arrived here. You heard what Jane said to Gino just now, Vance. She wasn't in love with you. And I'm sure you're not in love with her.'

Vance said stiffly,

'It's none of your business, Anthea. You don't know how I feel about Jane.'

178

There was a sound from behind Jane, a gentle creaking, as if Anthea had risen from the swing hammock. She heard her say softly, caressingly,

'I know *you*, Vance.'

There was a silence and then the sound of footsteps walking away. Jane glanced round and saw that Vance had gone, that there was no sign of Julian. She turned from the balcony and at the same moment Anthea said,

'Just a moment. There's something I'd like to say to you.'

She halted, aware of Anthea's narrowed green gaze on her.

'Yes?'

'I don't believe for one moment in this engagement of yours. I've got a very good idea why Vance brought you here, why there's this pretence of some association between you. It's because he doesn't want to hurt Julian. You see, I was once engaged to Vance, and Julian is still jealous of his brother.'

Jane steadied her voice.

'I know that. I mean, I know you and—and Vance were once engaged. He—told me.'

The green eyes flickered.

'He told you?' she shrugged. 'Then you understand the situation. Vance is still in love with me—did he tell you that too? And I'm still in love with him. We—were together in Athens.'

Jane felt pain stab her like a knife.

'I—I don't believe you.'

Again the shrug.

'Why should you care? You told Gino you weren't in love with Vance. I suppose that's true?'

'I don't believe Vance would do that to his brother.'

'My dear, you're crediting Vance with nobler motives than he possesses. He loves me, and as soon as Julian is well again we shall tell him the truth and ask for a divorce. I thought you'd better know now and then you can give up

179

this absurd pretence and go away from here. I really feel it would be better if you did. What a pity you couldn't have gone with your charming Italian friend. I mean, there he is with his yacht and everything.'

Jane said stammeringly,

'I—I can't believe anyone could be—be so—— Oh, it's not possible—you can't do this to—to your husband and to Judy. Vance wouldn't——' She broke off, unable to put into words the sense of despair and unhappiness that welled up in her.

'You see? There's really no point in your staying here. You don't like facing the facts of the situation.'

'You're right.' The words burst out from her. 'I don't want to stay. I couldn't stand it, it's all so hateful. Don't worry, I'll make arrangements to leave right away.'

'How sensible of you. And may I give you one more word of advice? I'm sure you wouldn't want any upsetting scenes for Julian, so I suggest you take your departure as unobtrusively as you can. Telephone for a taxi and go this afternoon when Julian and Judy will be resting and Vance will probably be working.'

Jane stared incredulously at the smoothly beautiful face before her, unable to believe that anyone could be so cold, so vindictive. Without another word she turned and almost ran from the terrace and through the sitting-room and up to her room.

She didn't believe the things Anthea had said of Vance, she couldn't, and yet, as she flung clothes and possessions into her suitcase, the snakelike doubts were emitting poison. She hated him, she hated Anthea; she was filled with sympathy for Julian, compassion for Judy.

Once she stopped in the midst of bundling up a sweater, almost on the point of rushing away to find Vance and confront him with Anthea's statements and demand if they were true. *Demand?* What business was it of hers? Vance owed *her* no allegiance, no honour. If the affection he had for his brother wasn't a deterrent, nothing Jane could say, no reproach she could make would stay his course.

Anthea had implied that she and Vance were lovers. Jane shivered as if with cold. It couldn't be true. But why should Anthea *say* such things if they were not?

It was none of her business, Jane told herself harshly. She had come here solely to pay off a debt, to act as a buffer between Vance and Anthea. She paused again, a hairbrush falling from cold and trembling fingers. As a buffer? No, as a blind, to gull Julian, so he would not realise what was happening between his wife and his brother.

She sat down on a chair, feeling almost sick with the confusion of emotions that raced through her. After some minutes she got a grip on herself and stood up and began to finish her packing. She wouldn't think about it; she would just act. Telephone for a taxi and make arrangements to leave the Villa. But where would she go?

To Athens? She could find out when the ferry left, it would be cheaper than the plane and she would go to Athens and see if she could find some temporary job. If she couldn't then she would have to return to England, probably overland, as the money she had with her would not be sufficient for an air ticket.

She glanced at her wrist-watch. It was lunch-time. If Vance was not in the study she would make the telephone call for a taxi and then somehow she would brace herself to endure the meal, to ignore Anthea's mocking gaze. In a little while after that, she would be gone.

Jane hardly knew how she got through lunch, but she made a pretext of eating and spoke only to Judy and Julian. When the meal was over she tried to make her escape, but before she could leave the room Vance cornered her by the door.

'I'd like to talk to you, Jane.'

Aware of Anthea's watchful eye upon them, she said in a low voice,

'I—I have a headache—I'm going upstairs to rest.'

He frowned.

'I'm sorry. Shall we say later—about four? In the study.'

She would be gone long before then. She nodded, knowing she was deceiving him.

'All right.'

She hurried upstairs and into her room. She had managed to telephone for a taxi and arranged for it to come at three o'clock. Surely by then the Villa would be quiet—Julian resting, Judy too. It didn't matter about Anthea—it was she who had instigated Jane's departure. Jane had decided to tell Hestia or any of the staff who might see her leaving that she was going into Corfu shopping. She had pushed her suitcase behind a bush in the garden so that no one would see her carrying it out. Now all that remained was to avoid Vance at all costs.

She was restless, pacing about the room, glancing at her wrist-watch from time to time. She went to the casement door and stared out at the garden, remembering the morning she had first seen it. It had been exciting, coming here with Vance, after their trip on the boat. Looking back it seemed as if she had already fallen under his spell.

Now she was leaving, without even saying goodbye. Was it only this morning that Gino had come here? How extraordinary to think that he was somewhere in the harbour of Corfu—even more extraordinary to realise that he had come all the way from Rome to find her and the gesture meant nothing to her. Once it would have been the answer to all her hopes and dreams. Perhaps in a little while she would feel the same way about Vance—feel that meeting him and falling in love had just been an interlude.

In a way it was easier to leave the Villa knowing he belonged to Anthea, but there was a bitterness to that knowledge, a sadness in thinking of the deception of Julian.

It was five past three, time to make tracks. Jane gave a last glance round the room and felt the ache of tears threaten. She picked up her shoulder bag and the thick ribbed cardigan she was taking for extra warmth and opening the bedroom door, peered out.

Everything was quiet. Almost on tiptoe she crept down the staircase and through the hall to the front door. As she gave another wary glance round she felt like a criminal stealing off with the household silver, and for a moment was tempted to walk boldly and noisily out into the courtyard. But the thought of meeting Vance stopped her and instead she went as quietly as she could across the paving to the drive, picking up the suitcase on her way. In another moment she was through the gateway and on to the road and safely out of view of the Villa.

Jane gave a sigh of relief and leant against the stone wall, feeling the rapid beating of her heart slowly subside. From where she stood she could both hear and see the taxi's approach and it would be a matter of seconds to hail it before it turned into the gateway of the Villa.

For ever. The words rang like a knell. She was leaving here for ever, for she knew that she would never return to the Villa Tyche or Corfu again. She couldn't bear the idea. She would never see Vance again, and the thought of that was even more unbearable.

She heard the faint humming of the car before she saw it—a black speck on the dusty road, coming nearer and nearer with every moment. She walked towards it, waving a hand to signal it and it slowed down, and as the small blackmoustached man leaned out she told him she was his intended passenger, and bumping the case up ahead of her, jumped in.

He turned his head to grin.

'You in hurries, no? Where you want taking?'

Jane bit her lip, not sure of her plans.

'The—the harbour, please. Where the ferries go from—the ones to Athens.'

He nodded, swinging the taxi round and setting off at a precipitate speed in the direction of Corfu. The road fell away behind them, the bay and the olive groves and the mountains, they rattled round the bends, bumping into sunken ruts where the surface had crumbled from the on-slaught of recent building lorries. Here the pines screened the sea, there a pink-washed villa, a blue-tiled roof hung above a rocky cove. And now Jane could see Pontikonisi, and she thought of the day they had gone in the boat to visit the small white chapel that crowned its summit. One per-fect day out of a string of other such days.

They had almost reached Corfu—soon the road would bend northwards round the town. The taxi was slowing down, the driver turning his head from time to time to look back, and Jane became aware of an incessant hooting from the horn of a car behind them. The taxi driver muttered something in Greek, some imprecation of wrath, and as he swung his own vehicle sideways so that, for a moment, it seemed to balance perilously on the few inches of roadway above the steep drop to the sea below, another car shot ahead of them and braked abruptly to a standstill some yards down the road.

Jane recognised the car even before a tall black-haired figure slid out and strode back to them. She sat bolt up-right, clutching at her shoulder bag as if for support, and felt her heart begin unaccountably to race.

The taxi door was pulled open, Vance's hand caught hold of her wrist. He said between gritted teeth,

'And where the devil to you think you're going?'

She found herself standing on the road, rubbing the wrist he had so painfully gripped.

'I—I'm going to Athens.'

'Like hell you are!' He broke off as the taxi-driver plunged between them, waving his hands, gesticulating wildly, shouting denunciations and calling upon St. Spiri-don to save him from such dangerous madmen as stood before him.

'I'm sorry,' Vance said, 'extremely sorry, but this was a—a matter of life and death. You understand? Of vital importance. I had to stop this lady taking her journey with you.' He pulled a wallet from his hip pocket and took out some notes. 'This is for your fare, and something for your trouble in the matter. I apologise again.'

The taxi-driver's scowl changed into a smile. He bowed his head, and then counted the notes, and after a moment, bowed again, an even deeper obeisance.

'Thank you, *kyrie*. I am much obliged to you.' He glanced at Jane and gave a third smaller bow and said '*kyria,*' before lifting out the suitcase on to the road. Then he swung himself into the driving seat and with a wide grin and a loud 'Good mornings' drove off.

'Well?' Vance demanded. 'What have you to say for yourself?'

'You've got a nerve,' Jane began furiously. 'How dare you come after me like this—interfere—pay off the taxi? What—what do you mean by it?'

'What do *you* mean by skulking off without a word to anyone, without any explanation—not even a goodbye?'

She said sullenly, 'Anthea knew I was leaving. And why.'

'Then perhaps you'll put *me* into the picture too.' He stopped to add frowningly, 'You've not changed your mind about Gino, for God's sake?'

'Of course not. I—oh, I can't explain. I—I just want to get away from the Villa, from Anthea and—and you.'

He said more gently, his slate grey eyes holding her glance,

'From Anthea, and from me. Not Julian—or Judy? We're to blame for your leaving so suddenly, and so secretly?' He reached out to take her hand. 'What is it—what have we done?'

She flung away his hand.

'You ask me that, after you stayed in Athens with Anthea? She told me—what—what happened.' The words seemed to force themselves out of her.

'Nothing happened.' He put a hand under her elbow and said, still in that quiet voice, 'Come and sit in the car. We've a lot to say to one another.'

'I don't know why——' she began, and then, under the

gentle pressure of his hand, allowed herself to be piloted along the road to the parked car.

He pulled open the door and dropped the case on to the back seat. When they were both in the car he turned to her.

'Now, what was all that about my staying with Anthea?'

Jane refused to look at him. She said in a muffled voice,

'She told me—she said you were—were still in love with her. That—that she was going to get a divorce from Julian.'

There was a pause of so long a duration that Jane found herself forced to look at Vance. The expression on his dark frowning face caused her heart to thump apprehensively. He said slowly,

'There is no question of a divorce.'

She waited for him to say something more, but when he didn't speak she said, with difficulty,

'Because of Julian, you mean?'

He looked at her, his grey eyes very direct.

'Because, quite apart from the fact that such a thing would kill Julian, I don't want to marry Anthea.' He took her hand in his. 'You do believe me when I say nothing "happened", as you put it, in Athens?' and as she nodded without speaking, her eyes on his face, he went on. 'It's difficult for me to talk about her without sounding a shyster. She came to the Grande Bretagne Hotel because she thought I was still in love with her. She told me she wasn't happy, that she had made a mistake in marrying Julian, and that it was obvious that I was going to make the same mistake if I married you. She added that she didn't take my engagement seriously.'

'She—she guessed that it was an—an arranged thing,' said Jane. 'She told me so, after Gino had been here. She said you had brought me to Corfu because you didn't want to hurt Julian and you—you were afraid of what might happen.'

He nodded slowly.

'That's true. At least, it was true. I was hesitant about

186

coming here because I wasn't sure how I felt about Anthea. A long time ago I was very much in love with her and I went on carrying this picture of her around in my mind. She was a measuring stick for other women. They never seemed as beautiful or as attractive or as fascinating as Anthea. Not surprising, for she is exceptionally lovely. No one can deny that.'

'No,' Jane said in a low voice.

His hold tightened on her fingers.

'But, you see, when I got here, it was all different. I was more interested in *you* than in Anthea. I think it all started when you were such a little fiend and crashed the car, and then, in the hospital at Cassino, you looked so small and pathetic in bed, with your arm trussed up and your leg in that cage thing. I found myself worrying about you—wanting to look after you. It was the first time in my life I'd wanted to cherish someone and not just make love to them.' He smiled slightly. 'That doesn't mean I *haven't* wanted to make love to you—I have. I wanted to kiss you, not as an act, but because I meant it.' He paused and put his other hand under her chin to tilt her face up towards him. 'Because I love you, Jane. Little dear Jane.'

She stared up at him, almost disbelievingly, despite the deep and tender note in his voice. What she saw in his eyes, a darker, warmer grey than they had ever been, must have convinced her. She gave a sigh, and said,

'Oh, Vance, I love you too.'

The next moment his mouth came down on hers and he was kissing her, and this time it was real. Utterly and wonderfully real. There was no more pretence, no more putting on an act for the benefit of onlookers. This was the thrilling, dizzying rapture of two people overwhelmingly in love with one another. Together, they were star-bound.

When at last Jane came back to earth it was to hear Vance say unsteadily, 'I was damnably jealous of Gino—it nearly choked me.'

She laid a finger against his mouth.

'I was jealous of Anthea. I still can't imagine why you should love me instead.'

'Can't you? Some day I'll tell you why, but right now it would be unfair to Anthea—she's come out of it too badly.'

Jane frowned hesitantly.

'Do we have to go back to the Villa?'

'Not immediately. Not if you don't want to.' He brushed a kiss on her hair, smoothing back the brown tresses with a gentle hand. 'You've a suitcase here—I can buy a toothbrush. Shall we go off somewhere and get married? I'm sure it can be arranged.'

Jane stared at him out of wide eyes.

'Oh, Vance!'

'Oh, Jane,' he mocked her lightly, then his voice sobered. 'I'm serious. I can phone Julian and tell him we're flying back to England to get a special licence and you can introduce me to your sister. What do you think of that idea?'

Jane sighed with happiness.

'Is it really possible? It sounds wonderful.'

'Then we'll do that.' His arms came about her and he pulled her close against him. 'But first of all, my precious Jane, I'm going to kiss you and tell you all over again how much I love you.'

FREE! *Harlequin Romance Catalogue*

Here is a wonderful opportunity to read many of the Harlequin Romances you may have missed.

The HARLEQUIN ROMANCE CATALOGUE lists hundreds of titles which possibly are no longer available at your local bookseller. To receive your copy, just fill out the coupon below, mail it to us, and we'll rush your catalogue to you!

Following this page you'll find a sampling of a few of the Harlequin Romances listed in the catalogue. Should you wish to order any of these immediately, kindly check the titles desired and mail with coupon.

Have You Missed Any of These
Harlequin Romances?

All books are 60c. Please use the handy order coupon.

DD

Have You Missed Any of These
Harlequin Romances?

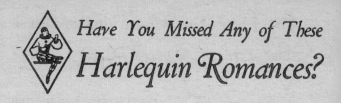
Have You Missed Any of These
Harlequin Romances?

All books are 60c. Please use the handy order coupon.

FF